The lights went on in St Angela's hospital, one by one, ward by ward. Day was beginning. To most of the patients, drugged with Mogadon, it seemed like the middle of the night. Some stirred resentfully, others slept determinedly on. It wouldn't be light for another hour or so yet. Then would be time enough to think of getting through the day, with its fears, hopes and above all, the boredom. To all of them, just being there signified some sort of crisis in their lives, great or small. The one reassuring element was the nurses, their angels, always there, dependable, cheerful, full of energy. They never seemed to have an off day, were never ill or tired. Nothing seemed to get them down. Angels, that's what they were. And they were stirring too, although it felt just as much like the middle of the night to them . . .

Nancy M Pherson.

Valerie Georgeson

Angels

Duty Calls

MAYFLOWER
GRANADA PUBLISHING
London Toronto Sydney New York

Published by Granada Publishing Limited
in Mayflower Books 1979
By arrangement with the British Broadcasting Association

ISBN 0 583 13199 6

A Mayflower Original
Copyright © Valerie Georgeson 1979
Copyright © Characters and format, BBC 1979

Granada Publishing Limited
Frogmore, St Albans, Herts AL2 2NF
and
3 Upper James Street, London W1R 4BP
866 United Nations Plaza, New York, NY 10017, USA
117 York Street, Sydney, NSW 2000, Australia
100 Skyway Avenue, Rexdale, Ontario, M9W 3A6, Canada
PO Box 84165, Greenside, 2034 Johannesburg, South Africa
CML Centre, Queen & Wyndham, Auckland 1, New Zealand

Set, printed and bound in Great Britain by
Cox & Wyman Ltd, Reading
Set in Monotype Times

Chapter One

The lights went on in St Angela's hospital, one by one, ward by ward. Day was beginning. To most of the patients, drugged with Mogadon, it seemed like the middle of the night. Some stirred resentfully, others slept determinedly on. It wouldn't be light for another hour or so yet. Then would be time enough to think of getting through the day, with its fears, hopes and above all, the boredom. To all of them, just being there signified some sort of crisis in their lives, great or small. The one reassuring element was the nurses, their angels, always there, dependable, cheerful, full of energy. They never seemed to have an off-day, were never ill or tired. Nothing seemed to get them down. Angels, that's what they were. And they were stirring too, although it felt just as much like the middle of the night to them . . .

First-Year Student, Anna Newcross, listened to the gurgles made by her four-year-old daughter, Emma, as she beat the living daylights out of her teddy-bear. Its squeaks of protest rent the peace of the early morning. She switched on her bedside light and yawned wearily. Might as well get up. At least she'd have plenty of time to sort the monster out, get her to the crèche and still make the day-shift on time. She crawled out of bed, registered the ache in the back of her legs and felt a passing moment of regret that she'd left Keith the tea-making machine along with everything else in their conjugal home.

Jean MacEwan, Casualty Sister, winced at the unearthly screech of her electric coffee grinder and vowed that tonight, she really would remember to grind the beans in advance.

Student Nurse Fleur Barrett, due on the same shift, turned over, moaning, and buried her face in the pillow, where she dreamt of the warm, spicy aroma of 'his' after-shave. Her nostrils flared and she sniffed appreciatively in her sleep. You could smell it in everything that belonged to him, even in the real leather upholstery of his new Porsche car. Ray . . .

In the Nurses' Home, Jay Harper, nervous about her first day on Casualty, groped her way round the room she shared with Pupil Nurse Rose Butchins, who wasn't on till late. Jay fell over Rose's shoes and saved herself by grabbing the bottom of her bed.

'For crying out loud, fairy feet!' Rose pulled the covers over her head, groaning, and Jay cursed.

It was a first day, too, for Beverley Slater, the young Jamaican girl; her first day on any ward at all. Her dream of tending the sick and wounded was about to become a reality. What would it be like? Ward G8, Female Geriatric. It didn't sound too promising. She wished she was back home with her family, where she belonged; wished she could see their familiar brown faces, smiling at her re-assuringly, telling her that everything was OK. She cleaned her teeth and bared her shining molars in the mirror.

'That's the warmest smile you'll see today, Sugar,' she told her reflection.

'Roll on coffee break and a currant bun,' thought the nurses going on duty. 'Oh, for a bite of breakfast cum supper and a bed,' thought the nurses going off. If they hurried, they might see their husbands for half an hour before they left to join the traffic queues over the bridge into London. 'Come on day-shift,' they urged.

Fleur saw three buses go as she turned the corner from her parents' flat. The cold, dark morning blunted her private dreams and put an edge on her outlook. She liked her job, but if only it could be more . . . flexible, bend itself more easily round her social life. Late nights and early mornings didn't go together but you've got to have a BIT of fun haven't you? That was her excuse, anyway. It was getting late, seven-fifteen ...

Anna's flat was just around the corner from the hospital, and she was up in plenty of time, but it had been a rush all the same; Emma's fault. It had been a battle royal with her this morning, first to get her cornflakes down her rather than down her nightie, then getting her dressed. It was the trousers that did it, sensible, drip-dry, dark-blue trousers. Emma wanted to wear her frock, the pretty one with the flowers embroidered in the corner that granny had given her.

But Anna knew that if she did, she'd get it ruined at the crèche, when they played that game of hurling their dinners at each other. Well, that's what it looked like they got up to anyway, judging by the state of their clothes by the end of the day. Anna won, and dragged her daughter out of the flat suitably dressed in trousers, in plenty of time for the shift.

It was when they reached the corner of the street that Emma started howling. Anna looked at her daughter, wondering, not for the first time, how so many decibels could issue from such a tiny little frame. But the look gave way to one of despair, as she realized Em'd wet her pants. Anna whisked her daughter back to the flat to change her into the pretty dress shouting, 'You're determined to make me late, aren't you?'

'I don't know how you cope,' said her neighbour, cowering out of reach on the corner of the stairs, as Anna flew back up to her flat, shouting. 'Sorry if she woke you!'

The crèche was already half-filled with nurses' children, when at last Anna led Emma through the door. The sun had risen, and its angry red light streamed past the animal cut-outs on the windows, casting strange shadows on the groups, boys on one side, girls on the other, like two tribes ready for

7

jungle warfare. Emma let go her mother's hand and tottered to the centre of the room where, Graham, her little friend stood smiling uncertainly at her. The other children dropped their toys and watched tensely as the pair drew closer, came to a halt and sized one another up. Emma's hip drooped insolently, inviting Graham to relax those steely muscles in his wary little legs. He smiled again. Suddenly Emma lunged forward and began kicking the hell out of his shins.

'Atta girl,' thought Anna. The little boy winced manfully for a while then burst into tears amid the high-pitched jeers and laughter of a satisfied audience.

The din brought Edith Radley, the crèche nurse, scurrying from the kitchen.

'Stop it. Stop it at once.' The nurse glared at Anna. 'Why didn't you stop her?' she challenged. 'You're her mother.'

'Why? Let them sort it out.' Nurse Radley stared incredulously. 'It's the Year of the Child, Children's Rights and all that. Who are WE to interfere?'

'Well, really! It's no wonder she's turning into a tomboy ... no wonder at all!'

'Nonsense' Anna retorted, delighted at the effect she was producing. 'There's nothing unfeminine about aggression.' Anna smiled at the bobbing curls on her daughter's head as she, totally aware of her utterly feminine power, stomped off into a corner with a great display of ignoring the little boy. He stood pathetic, and lost, in the middle of the room, shunned by boys and girls alike. It was unbearable. He'd do anything to put things right. He'd even offer up his tender shins once again, to her little yellow bootees. Gingerly he approached the girl. Emma turned on him, arms akimbo.

'What do you want, Graham?' she yelled. Graham rubbed his shin and smiled.

'That hurt.'

'Good,' said Emma and obligingly the fatal bootee struck again.

'Serve him right the little fool,' said Anna. 'Teach him to fend for himself.' Nurse Radley, comforting the victim, stared at this mother with narrowed eyes. Mothers didn't usually talk like that. Not to her anyway.

'Oh, of course,' she said, smiling at Anna, 'we must remember, Emma comes from a broken home, mustn't we?'

'Cow,' thought Anna.

'I try to teach them to make love, not war.' Nurse Radley was proud of that. Anna looked at the kids, playing their treacherous game together.

'What's the difference?' she said and turning on her heel, stomped out, every inch her daughter's mother.

As Anna flew on to Male Surgical just in time to save herself from a black look, Jean MacEwan looked at the clock in Casualty, sighed, and rang Administration.

'Has Nurse Barrett reported in sick?' Nurse Barrett had NOT reported in sick ... but since Sister MacEwan was short staffed she could borrow Nurse Frost from A. & E. unless Charge Nurse Russell had a sudden rush on.

Satisfied, Jean took her new student nurse, Jay Harper, on a tour of the department. It was a lot to take in. Jay looked nonplussed.

'Don't worry,' Jean explained, 'there's always somebody qualified around to help. If in doubt ask.' Jean remembered her first day on Casualty as a student, the fear that someone would bleed to death before her very eyes, or suffer cardiac arrest and she would be left on her own to cope. 'Nurses in Casualty carry far more responsibility than they ever do on the wards ... but you'll get to like that once you've been here for a while. All the nurses do.'

Jay looked doubtful. She knew that with the first emergency all she'd ever been taught would fly straight out of her head.

'There's one thing,' Jean added, 'it's quite exciting. We never know what's going to happen next.'

Up on Ward G8, Beverley Slater was being given the run down by acting sister, Staff Nurse Bowell. 'You'll find this ward very unpredictable, Nurse Slater.'

Beverley warmed at the 'Nurse' Slater, she felt she had status at last.

'But,' Staff went on, 'things can get out of hand pretty quickly if you're not on your toes. It's them against us. That's how I look at it.' There was a pause. Nurse Bowell stared at Beverley's frizzy hair under her paper hat, and at the eyes. There was a wild look in them. Fear thought Nurse Bowell. 'It's your very first ward isn't it?'

Beverley nodded.

'Oh dear' Staff sighed. It seemed it was a crime to be on your first ward. Beverley tried hard not to feel guilty. 'I'd better ring for help . . . we'll never manage without.' Nurse Bowell appealled to her auxiliary, Nurse Jarmolinski, standing firm as a rock by Beverley's side, then rang Admin. Nurse Jarmolinski was a Pole, middle-aged, and comfortable in shape and outlook. She liked working for the old dears on the ward, she was very religious and proud as punch of the new Pope. She was saving to go to Rome next Easter. Nurse Bowell, waiting at the end of the line for Admin. to come up with extra staff, eyed the crucifix round the auxiliary's neck, then turned away to write down a name. 'Anna Newcross, First-Year Student'. The auxiliary took the chance to twist the cross to the back of her neck, so that only the chain showed. She was a great believer in avoiding trouble.

Beverley edged closer to her. She seemed a haven in time of crisis.

'Relief forces are on the way,' Nurse Bowell beamed, 'even if it is only a student.' Her eyes glanced over the chain on the auxiliary's wrinkled neck. 'Aha,' she thought, 'she's turned it round to the back . . . crafty!' But she said nothing. Nurse Bowell liked to play a waiting game. She addressed the auxiliary with a smile. 'You'll keep an eye on Nurse Slater won't you, Nurse?'

'Yes, Staff.' Nurse Jarmolinski knew her place.

Acting Sister Bowell then turned back to Beverley. 'There's a rough guide to ward routine on the notice board here . . . we find if we stick to it, in face of all opposition we can just about get through. They like it and we like it. That way we all know exactly where we are. The thing to do is to keep one jump ahead of them. You'll get to know their little foibles quite quickly, I'm sure.'

'Them and us,' thought Beverley. The teachers in the school had said that theirs was a caring profession. Where was the caring here?

Nurse Bowell was rattling off the day's routine. 'After we've got them sat up, we give them tea, then it's washing, dressing and toileting. After that, breakfast, bedmaking, medicine-round and observations, patients' coffee, toileting. Doctors' rounds are usually Tuesdays and Thursdays otherwise dressings followed by patients' lunch and toileting. The afternoon includes visits by and to physiotherapists, occupational therapy, chiropodist, hairdresser, etc. Then we finish outstanding dressings and toileting. If possible we set aside an hour for socializing with the patients, then there's medicine-round again, observations, etc., patients' tea and er . . .' Her eyes searched the list on the wall.

Beverley volunteered a wild guess. 'Toileting?'

Nurse Bowell glared at her. 'Yes,' she said. 'That's right.

In one end and out the other is the general rule. Then with any luck we can usually get them back in bed before any further calamities. All right?'

Beverley smiled weakly and tried to remember how you were supposed to hold a non-ambulant patient. Old people have brittle bones. What if one fell and broke a leg while she was supporting her?

Beverley shivered and was glad to see a relaxed, confident smile on the auxiliary's face. Nurse Jarmolinski was congratulating herself on having got away with her cross and chain. Acting-Sister Bowell turned to the Kardex system to read the reports of night staff on the patients' progress. It was impossible for Beverley to take it all in at once, but when Staff asked her if everything was clear . . . daring her to say 'No' . . . Beverley answered, 'Yes, thank you, Staff Nurse Bowell.'

The auxiliary suppressed a smile and the staff nurse saw it. 'Staff will do,' she explained to her pupil nurse, 'but in future, if you address me by my full name, kindly remember that the name is Bowell . . . understand? Bow as in bow and arrow.'

Beverley bit her lip and vowed she'd remember.

'I think that's about it,' said Staff. 'Oh, don't forget to record all incontinence on the separate card system . . .'

Beverley's heart sank. Incontinence. It was all very well changing the nappies of your younger brother and sister . . . but old ladies! That was different.

Nurse Bowell gave the battle cry, 'Off you go and the best of British.'

Beverley stuck so close to the auxiliary she almost tripped her up on the way out of the office. But the acting-sister hadn't finished yet. 'Oh, and Nurse Jarmolinski . . .' she said casually, 'I've told you before about that crucifix.'

The auxiliary, defeated, took the offending jewellery from

12

her neck and Nurse Bowell smiled a secret smile. No one could get the better of her.

It was after eight when Fleur rolled into Casualty. Sister MacEwan was all right, she wouldn't mind just this once. Fleur was a good nurse, and got on well with the Casualty Sister. Jean saw her come in and her eyes asked the question. 'Why so late?'

'Sorry, Sister,' said Fleur, 'I overslept and then I had to wait ages for a bus.'

Jean smiled. 'Happens to the best of us,' she said. She looked at the nurse's eyes. Her black face had even blacker rings under the eyes. Always considerate of her nurses' welfare, Jean asked, 'Did you have a good night, last night?'

Fleur grinned, remembering the episode in Epping Forest after the disco closed. 'Yeah,' she said, 'great.' But her face fell when she realized the sister had been referring to the quality of her sleep.

Jean nodded. 'I see,' she said, and walked away, leaving Fleur to bite off the end of her tongue.

An auxiliary nurse is an assistant to the nurses, but if anything, Beverley was glad to be assistant to the auxiliary this morning. The older nurse took her round the ward, sitting the patients up. It seemed a shame to break into their dreams, shouting, 'Wakey wakey. Time for your tea.' But their patients had already had a long lie-in compared with those on the other wards. They approached Mrs Saunders' bed and roused the old lady. She stared at them vacantly, focusing with difficulty on Beverley's strange brown face.

'You're new,' she managed to gasp as the nurses heaved her into a sitting position. The auxiliary tucked her handbag in beside her, like a teddy bear, and Beverley turned away, her stomach heaving.

'You'll get used to it, my darling,' the auxiliary encouraged her. 'Hold your breath.' The smell of stale urine came as a shock to Beverley. She put her hand to her mouth and made a dash for the sluice room, passing Nurse Bowell on the way. The staff nurse shook her head and sighed, taking over from her on the round. Nurse Jarmolinski's heart sank. She knew what was coming; the long complaint about the hysterectomy the year before, how she shouldn't be heaving patients about like this, and how Bob would have a fit if he could see her now. Nurse Bowell liked complaining. Suddenly she stopped before an empty bed and frowned. 'Shouldn't there be someone in that bed?' she asked. She looked at the name on the bottom. 'Martha Poole' it read.

The controlled madness of the day on G8 had begun. Martha, now almost a permanent resident on the ward and 'confused', was even then ambling down the hospital corridors, her stockings round her ankles, muttering furiously to herself. 'I don't want your sausages. You know what you can do with your sausages. If you're not careful I'll tell you where you can stick your sausages. One by one.' She was out in the street before the porters caught her up, laying into a passer-by about those sausages.

Nurse Bowell and Nurse Jarmolinski heard the tale over the phone from the head porter and laughed and laughed.

'Well, my darling,' said the auxiliary, wiping away the tears, 'if you didn't laugh, you'd cry!' So they laughed. But Anna Newcross, reporting for duty, was not impressed when she saw nurses lounging on the office desk, giggling for all they were worth. Nurse Bowell regarded the newcomer.

'I'm told you're run off your feet.' Anna's voice was accusing, and Nurse Bowell took an instant dislike to her.

'So we are, Nurse.'

Anna was furious. She was a student, supposed to be learning her job. She had spent the last week in school being

14

taught how to care for patients on a male surgical ward. She was now supposed to be practising what she'd learnt and here she was instead, being shoved about from pillar to post just because this nurse said she was short-staffed. Well she didn't look it!

'I'm supposed to be on Male Surgical' she said.

'I'm aware of that, Nurse' came the sharp reply. 'You must simply try to look on your stay with us as a pleasant surprise!' Nurse Bowell smiled sweetly at the belligerent student.

Anna glared at her. 'How long will you be needing me?' she insisted.

Nurse Bowell looked at her well-trimmed nails then at Anna. 'I really couldn't say, Nurse. But I must ask you to remember, that on THIS ward, patients come first.'

Anna swallowed her anger. 'Sorry, Sister.'

'Perhaps you'll help the auxiliary with the breakfasts?' Nurse Jarmolinski jumped to it. She knew that sharp sweetness in her superior's voice. It meant, 'Get back in your box'. Nurse Jarmolinski got back in her box, and Anna followed her on to the ward.

'Cheap labour,' she fumed. 'That's what we are. I don't know why they call us "students" at all! Just cheap labour!' Nurse Bowell watched the rebel go.

'One step out of line,' she thought. 'That's all. Just one step!' She gave the student's back a mean look.

Anna's stomach was rumbling. She hadn't had time for breakfast. All she'd had was the soggy remains of Em's cornflakes. She yearned for the patients' sausage and bacon.

Martha's was cold, stuck to the plate in its own congealed fat by the time they wheeled the old lady back on to the ward. What a waste! Anna resented it bitterly, lying there, looking at her while she and Beverley 'tidied' Martha up. Her stockings hung like lisle sacks about her ankles.

15

Beverley, rather flustered, looked helplessly round the ward for a stray suspender or something as Anna searched in Martha's locker.

Suddenly there was pandemonium. First of all, Martha accused Anna of stealing from her, then she started shouting at Mrs Saunders, 'You've pinched them, haven't you! You've pinched me garters!'

Mrs Saunders denied the charge vehemently, but the garters could still not be found. The nurses were forced to make new ones, which, if it did not placate Martha, did at least keep her stockings up. It was quite a performance trying to fit the elastic round the old lady's legs. Suddenly overcome with a sense of the ridiculous, Anna and Beverley burst into laughter, the elastic pinged from Martha's leg and they ended on the floor, rolling about, helpless with laughter. It was mad ... quite mad, and nothing whatsoever like Anna had been led to expect on Male Surgical.

The aroma of bacon and egg sweetened the air of the canteen. Bob Stetchley took the chewing gum from his mouth and grinned as the woman behind the counter piled the last of the bacon on to his plate. He gave her an appreciative wink.

'Got to keep up my strength.'

'Get on,' she turned, blushing, for all her fifty years, to the next in the queue, Anna.

'Bacon and eggs, please,' she said.

'Breakfast's off. It's half past.'

Anna glared at the woman and cast a greedy eye over Bob's generous plateful.

'What's he got then?'

'It's half past.' Bob, sensing a storm brewing behind him, looked back. The nurse was seething, but the woman wouldn't budge.

'You can have toast,' she said.

'All right,' Anna threatened. 'Toast. Two slices.'

Bob smiled, paid for his breakfast and the rest of his crowd made a space for him at their table. Anna, coffee and toast in hand, was searching for a place to sit, when she caught Bob staring frankly at her.

'God,' she thought, 'you don't half fancy yourself, mate.' She gave his plate a meaningful look then turned contemptuously away.

Barry Hodgson, following Bob's gaze, caught the look. 'What's bugging her?'

'I got her breakfast,' Bob grinned.

'Bad-tempered little bitch!'

'Yeah.' Bob watched the flaring nostrils and burning eyes as they singled out an empty corner table where she could sit in solitary contemplation of the butter melting into her pieces of plain toast. 'Shame.' He liked the determined turn of the head and the way she swung her hips into the seat. 'Just needs breaking in,' he said.

'Fancy your chances?' Barry challenged him.

'Yeah.'

'What's the odds?'

'Make her by the end of . . .' Looking at her, Bob's nerve faltered. 'Next week,' he said.

'You're on.' Barry's fiver hit the table. He stared across the canteen, sizing her up. 'I bet it'll take a month.'

Anna, uncomfortable under male scrutiny, suddenly turned and purposefully caught their eyes. Unembarrassed she looked them up and down and saw the fivers on the table between them. A sudden impulse made her give a provocative tilt to her head as she averted her eyes and spread the butter. She was almost smiling.

Bob winked at his colleague. 'Want to change your bet?' he said, and picking up his plate of bacon, wove his way between the tables to Anna's side. 'Fancy a bit of bacon between them slices?' he asked.

'How much?'

'To you, sweetheart? Nothing.'

'Ha ha,' said Anna.

'Aren't you going to ask me to sit down?'

'What's the point? You will anyway.'

Bob shrugged and sat, arms folded on the table, staring straight into her face. Carefully Anna arranged the bacon between the slices.

'Cheers,' she said.

'Cheers.' They smiled at each other. Bob's confidence was growing.

'How much did you lay on me?' said Anna.

The squash-playing, rugger-jostling shoulders sagged visibly, and Anna bit into the sandwich with satisfaction.

'Hey, that's not fair.'

'All's fair in love and war.'

'You asked for it,' Bob threatened, and reached for his chewing gum like a lifebelt.

'You work in the path. lab. don't you?'

'Yeah ... microbiologist.'

Anna nodded. 'Bright are you?'

'So-so ... I got a first.'

Anna acted impressed. 'First-class mind, eh?'

Bob smiled, pleased.

'But only in one direction.' Anna smiled now. She enjoyed popping his balloons. She waited for the next approach, wondering what it would be. He was thinking. Well, she was glad she'd made him think, anyway. She'd hate to be an unworthy opponent for this first-class mind, in one direction only ... on the other hand, Anna eyed him as frankly as he had done her, his body was first-class in several directions.

'What are you doing tonight?' she asked.

'Washing my hair,' he said.

Anna smiled and waited.

'No . . . got a court booked.' He chewed on his gum like a man determined to stand his ground.

'Tennis?' she asked.

'Squash,' he answered.

'Ah yes,' Anna nodded. 'I might have known you'd play a faster game.'

Bob stared after her as Anna left the canteen. He'd laid a fiver on that woman. He began to wonder if she was worth it . . . he needed new squash balls. Damn her! She'd gone and lit a spark in him he couldn't put out. He'd give Barry Hodgson one hell of a pasting tonight. He shuffled restlessly in his seat and mentally sent the ball cracking against the wall and wham smash through his opponent's defences.

Chapter Two

The 137 was just leaving Gipsy Hill as Anna got back to the ward. Mrs Carr paid her fare to Streatham, moaning about the cost. She was feeling unwell that morning, a little flushed.

'Half-fare, please ... like children,' said Mrs Carr apologetically. The conductress took the fare, checked the pensioner's pass card and went upstairs. She'd not managed to get up there since Crystal Palace.

On Ward G8, Anna, feeling better after her successful encounter with Bob Stetchley, got stuck into the bedmaking, whipping soiled sheets from under Beverley's nose before she'd even had time to register the smell and Staff commented bleakly, 'If this keeps up we might get through the day without further disaster ... barring accident of course.'

Nurse Jarmolinski looked at the two empty beds on the ward and put in a prayer that they stay that way ... at least for today.

They were well past Streatham, circling Clapham Common when the passenger on Mrs Carr's left, shifted uneasily, looked warily at the seat, then shuffled off to a vacant place further down the bus. Mrs Carr's nose was running with suppressed tears. The conductress coming down the stairs, tried to remember which stop the old woman had asked for. She looked at her face. She seemed upset, confused.

'Gone past your stop, have you?' she asked.

'No ... no, I'm not there yet.'

'Are you sure? We're at Clapham now.'

'No ... no, I paid to the terminus,' Mrs Carr insisted. 'I should know.'

'All right.' The conductress thought she was trying to get away with it, pulling a fast one. Some of these pensioners had to be watched! Mrs Carr became aware of the other passengers. Their eyes turned in her direction rather too often. One woman frankly stared at her. What was the matter with them? Didn't they know it was rude to stare? Mrs Carr swayed with the bus. Heat rose up her spine and crept over her skull bathing her eyes in sweat. Pain receded and a feeling of nausea overcame her.

Her hanky covered her mouth, and the staring eyes were confused into a nightmare of voices and hands that touched her. She thrashed out, her arms flying in all directions and the bus came to a halt. A woman's voice came through the haze, loud and distinct. 'She's wet herself, poor old soul.' The cockney shrill echoed in Mrs Carr's brain like an accusation. 'She's wet herself. She's wet herself.' She began to cry and the comforting arms were no comfort.

It had been a quiet morning in Casualty. Jay was relieved and disappointed at the same time. She'd expected drama; life and death. All she'd had were cuts and bruises, and Fleur had taught her to bandage a sprain. Fleur knew the ropes. She'd been on Casualty for a few weeks. Jay admired her confidence and wished she could be like her, easy going; she talked to the patients like she'd known them all her life; And they responded. It was easy to see how she got on with men. She lived a double life, did Fleur. Jay wondered if she ever had the time to sleep! So, it was natural, when the bus stopped outside the hospital gates, that Jay should be the one left behind to set up the dressings' trolley while Fleur and Ron went with the porter to deal with the old lady from the bus.

Mrs Carr was trembling but still capable of resistance when

the porter took her arm and guided her into the wheelchair. Everyone was shouting at her. A black nurse peered into her face and yelled. 'You'll be all right now, love!' Mrs Carr put her hands to her ears. Then a young man came to help; she heard him ask what had happened, then the black nurse laughed and said, 'She wet herself, on the bus!'

'No, No!' The old lady protested violently.

The young man in the white jacket looked at her, took her handkerchief from her hands, put it to her nose and shouted, 'Blow!' Mrs Carr looked at him. If he hadn't been such a nice-looking young man she might have objected, but as it was . . . She blinked at him and blew.

'Where were you going?' he shouted.

'To the vet's,' she shouted back. The black nurse and the young man looked at each other.

'Don't you mean to the doctor's?' asked the young man.

Mrs Carr sighed, and knowing that resistance was useless, allowed them to wheel her into the hospital.

On G8 Anna shouted into an old lady's face, 'Have you finished?' A startled look told of interrupted dreams. Anna peered at her, tray in hand, waiting.

'Yes.' Mrs Saunders retreated fretfully back into her past and Anna removed the half-eaten lunch. Close by, Mrs Lilley was sitting with her husband who was visiting from the male ward. They sat there not looking, not speaking. They'd been together for fifty years and now for the first time they were sleeping in separate beds. From time to time Mr Lilley wept and she would pat his arm. He couldn't sleep without her. 'I miss her bum, ye see,' he'd explain. 'I curl round it, you know . . . I miss that.'

Anna looked at his wasted body. She wondered if it had ever been first-class. The old people around her had a strange effect on Anna. They made her feel young and fit and full of life. Yes ... and determined to live it too. She felt much better than she had done this morning. 'Live now,' she thought. Mrs Betts 'in' to give her relatives a rest was clamouring for the telly. Anna switched it on and every head turned like clockwork to the screen; living life at second-hand. Well, they had no choice, but she had. She was going to make sure she lived life to the full. First-hand.

The details of Mrs Carr's life were proving difficult to ascertain. She glared resentfully at Fleur. 'What do you want to know for?' she demanded.

'For the records,' Fleur pleaded. 'Is your husband alive?'

'No,' Mrs Carr said emphatically. 'Please can I go now? I have to collect his pills, he's very ill you know.' First-Year Student Nurse Frost decided to have a go.

'Don't you mean your pills?'

'No, I do not! Tristran's! He's a West Highland terrier and he has a heart murmur.'

Fleur raised her eyebrows and changed tack. 'First name, please,' she demanded, pen poised.

Nurse Frost smiled at the old lady. She seemed to like him. 'I'm Ron,' he said.

Mrs Carr simpered, 'Anne.'

'How do you do?'

'How do you do?' They were getting on swimmingly.

'Address?'

Mrs Carr, irritated at the interruption of their budding relationship, snapped, 'That's my affair.'

Fleur sighed. Really it was hopeless.

'Who's your doctor then?'

Mrs Carr saw no reason to withhold the name of her GP, and relieved, Fleur wrote it down. Now came the tricky bit; her age. Fleur looked at Ron and laughed, 'Date of birth?'

Ron smiled, took a deep breath and laying on all the

23

charm he asked, 'When were you born, love?' Mrs Carr's look turned him to stone.

They would get no more from her now. Sister Jean put a call through to Dr Gould and Ron wheeled her straight into the treatment room. Mrs Carr was beginning to enjoy being wheeled about. Ron manoeuvred the vehicle with skill, and gratefully she looked in her purse for a five p piece, handing it to him with all the grace of the Queen Mother. 'Thank you orderly.'

Ron grinned. 'It's all right, it's free . . . on the National Health.'

The five p was dropped back into the purse and Mrs Carr was surprised on looking up to find the young man still standing there.

'Yes?' she queried.

'We have to help you get undressed . . . for examination.'

'You?' she stared at him in disbelief. 'You're an orderly!'

'You know I'm very hurt you think that,' Ron exchanged a glance with Fleur standing behind him (he was enjoying this), 'most people think I'm a doctor because of the white coat.'

Mrs Carr gave him a hard look. She was not to be taken in. 'Doctors don't push wheelchairs,' she said emphatically.

Ron retreated, admitting defeat, and left the old lady to the capable Nurse Barrett.

He was talking with Sister Jean and the Casualty doctor when they heard the screams. Sister Jean actually ran to the treatment room, closely followed by Ron, and flung the curtains aside. Mrs Carr was very upset, crying out, 'Leave me alone . . . take your hands off me.' And Fleur in a fury was shouting at the old lady for all she was worth, 'Stupid cow! Black's not dirty . . . I bet my hands are a lot cleaner than yours, you filthy white trash!'

'Nurse Barrett.' Jean's voice cut through the uproar and

Fleur, helpless with fury, turned to her as though appealing for justice.

'She said "take your dirty hands off me".'

Mrs Carr denied it and the argument was about to start again when Sister Jean sent Fleur out of the room. The old lady was shaking. She tried to speak but the words came out like hiccups, spasmodically.

'I didn't say . . . they were . . . dirty.' It was all so terrible, such a fuss. Mrs Carr hated fusses. 'I have no colour prejudice,' she explained to Jean. 'None at all. How could the child think such a thing!'

When Jay came to sit with her, Mrs Carr was calmer. She asked if there was anyone they could send for, to be with her. Mrs Carr looked at the young nurse. There was a gap of more than sixty years between them. Mrs Carr had been through two world wars, a marriage, poverty, sickness. The nurse was only just beginning. And yet as the old lady knew, the young look down on the old with all the self-confidence of youth, dismissing them as has-beens or never-weres. The nurse touched the old lady's hand and Mrs Carr looked at her. The face was young, yes and the voice was English, but there was something Asian about the face. She had that gentle shyness that Indian women have, the soft eyes so vulnerable and yet so disarming.

'Isn't there anyone at all?'

Perhaps she would understand. Years of suspicion and distrust were broken down in seconds . . .

'No,' she said, 'not since James died.' The eyes waited. They wanted more. Mrs Carr went on, 'It's twenty years ago now . . . how old are you?'

'Nineteen.'

The old and the young woman looked at each other.

'Have you any children?'

'No,' Mrs Carr shook her head. 'How could we? We

were like brother and sister. Our what I believe you call "intimate relations" were severely curtailed by my complaint you see.'

Jay tilted her head and the eyes looked puzzled.

'Infections of the waterworks,' Mrs Carr explained.

Jay nodded.

'You must be very lonely,' she said and sensing a point of contact, warmed to her.

But the reply was unexpected. 'Not really. People can be such a nuisance, don't you think? I can do as I like you see. And there's Tristan . . .

'Your dog?'

'He has a heart murmur. I was on my way to the vet's for his pills when I . . . became indisposed.' Mrs Carr shuffled on the couch.

'Are you uncomfortable?' Jay asked.

Mrs Carr's answer was more precise. 'I am in pain.'

'I'm sorry.' Mrs Carr saw that Jay was telling the truth. 'If you would let the doctor examine you, I'm sure he could help.'

'They haven't helped me in the past.' Mrs Carr seemed determined.

'Won't you let him try?' The old lady did not answer. The pain was finally wearing down her resistance.

'Why won't you undress?'

The wrinkled hands covered the face. 'I'm so ashamed.'

'Why? What of?'

'My underneaths.' The old lady whimpered. Jay managed to hide her astonishment. 'I haven't changed them since last Friday . . .'

On the ward, Beverley was finding a point of contact with another old lady, Mrs Betts, or Granny Betts as she had begun to call her. She was a bit of home to her, always ready

26

for a laugh or a sing. All she needed was a brown face. She was a bit of Jamaican sunshine in this pale outpost of Western life. The grey faces of those who had given up, or had been given up. She clung to her and to the Polish auxiliary, like she had clung to her mother as a child. She knew that Granny Betts had a grand-daughter, a nurse, like her, and resented the grand-daughter on behalf of the old lady, feeling she had let her down.

'No wonder Britain's sinking,' she said. 'You've got no sense of what's right . . . no sense of community . . . you'd not get the old people shoved on the scrap heap in Jamaica!'

'People have got to live their own lives,' said Anna. 'You can't molly-coddle them all the time.'

Beverley looked at her in disgust. 'I think you're terrible,' she said. 'You just don't care.'

'Oh, shut up and do something useful.'

Anna handed her a glass of water . . . 'Try and get Martha Poole to have a drink or she'll never get any better. And that's what we're here for, to get them to stand on their own feet!'

Beverley took the glass of water and went, smouldering, into the day room. She put the glass to Martha's lips and with a sudden movement Martha upset the lot all over her. The nurse stood dripping in the sluice room. Anna, going off duty, was cheered at the sight. 'There's life in the old girl yet,' she said.

Jay stood by the bed in the treatment room as Doctor Choudry examined the notes. Mrs Carr sat in a hospital gown, her clothes wrapped discreetly in a plastic bag at her feet, and a thermometer jutting from her mouth. The doctor glanced up and caught Jay's eye. His look was a bit too direct. Jay flushed, and took the thermometer from the patient's mouth. 'Thirty-nine point five,' she read.

'Yes. It is rather high,' Dr Choudry commented. 'I think we'll need a sample for the path. lab.' Sister Jean pointed to Jay's notes.

'You'll see Nurse Harper tested a sample after Dr Gould's examination . . . and one has also been sent to the path. lab.' Dr Choudry looked at Jay again. She held his look but it was an effort. She shuffled uncomfortably and suppressed an urge to grin all over her face.

'Good girl,' he said. Then ignoring Mrs Carr, the young Pakistani doctor addressed the sister. 'Is she allergic to anything do we know?'

Mrs Carr, freed of the thermometer, spoke up. 'I tolerate penicillin and tetracycline very well but am allergic to sulphonamides.'

Doctor Choudry took Mrs Carr in for the first time. There was a look of surprise on his face, as he apologized.

Mrs Carr went on. 'My bladder may not be functioning properly, Doctor, but my intellect and my hearing remain unimpaired.'

Doctor Choudry smiled and swallowed hard as he approached the bed.

'Are you going to let us help you, dear lady?'

Mrs Carr felt herself weakening. Her little girl voice responded to the charm; she looked from the doctor to the nurse. 'You people do have a way with you,' she said.

Jay, an Anglo Asian, and surprised to be classed with Doctor Choudry, suddenly looked at him. He had his arm round the old lady surreptitiously feeling her kidneys. 'Ah, but we're all the same under the skin, don't you agree?' he said.

Mrs Carr smiled. 'No I don't,' she said. 'And it's not a bad thing either.'

He patted her arm and let her go, arranging with Sister to take her in. Mrs Carr had been wooed to submission. Jay

28

understood her feelings. In her place she'd have felt the same. There was definitely something about those eyes. Suddenly the doctor turned and asked, 'Have you ever suffered from incontinence before?'

The old body stiffened and quickly Jay put in, 'No. Never.'

Her look warned the doctor off. He only just managed to stop himself saying 'sorry' before he stepped through the curtains Sister Jean held open for him.

'A really excellent nurse that Nurse Harper,' he said. 'I'm most impressed.'

Mrs Carr looked at Jay's dazed face and said, 'Rather a nice man, don't you think?'

Jay, shaken out of a dream, turned to the old lady and smiled at the knowing look. 'Mrs Carr!' she said.

Anna, on a split shift, had gone off duty when the call came up to the ward. Concerned about the old lady and feeling she had been upset quite enough for one day, Sister Mac-Ewan rang acting-sister on G8, Sister Bowell, to warn her of the new admission.

'She can be a bit difficult,' said Jean. 'She needs careful handling.'

'So she doesn't think I can cope,' thought Nurse Bowell, as she put the phone down. Gathering her nurses together, she warned them of the new admission ... 'This one's a troublemaker,' she told them.

Chapter Three

Anna should have gone to pick up Emma first but there was the shopping to do and she could get through it ten times quicker without that little hoodlum trailing along behind her all the time. Nurse Radley could cope for a little while longer and serve her right. Anna flew round the shops and ransacked the supermarket in the hope of finding something that Em would actually eat. Spaghetti shaped like bears did not fool her little daughter. As usual she ended up with too much to carry and was very relieved to see the familiar shape of a male nurse as she lugged her bags along the street.

It was Ron. Ron Frost. Anna smiled. Ron was lost, staring into a shop window, miles away, like any child in a toy shop. What was he looking at? Anna approached quietly from behind and looked over his shoulder. It was a Newton's Cradle. Someone had set the balls in motion and Ron was following the inevitable movements, transfixed.

'Wait till you're a charge nurse,' Anna said.

Ron saw her reflection in the window, smiled and turned to her. 'Can I carry your shopping?' he asked obligingly.

'You're an angel,' said Anna, handing it over. 'You on a split shift too?'

'Yes.'

'Pain, isn't it?'

'I don't mind.'

'Why aren't you in your little cell in the Nurses' Home studying . . . or something?' Ron flushed and Anna laughed.

'It's a bit noisy for that . . . builders are in.'

'Ah. You can come home with me if you like ... after I've picked up Emma.'

Ron looked at Anna. It sounded more like a command; she was so sure of herself. He idly wondered if she was making a pass, but there'd be Emma after all, and he hadn't anything better to do.

'Thanks,' he said. The shopping was getting heavy. Anna saw and slackened her pace.

'I didn't ask you just so's you'd carry my shopping, you know.'

Ron's smile said, 'Didn't you?'

Emma made for her mother like a train when she saw her, moaning about the repression of Nurse Radley. 'She's 'orrible,' said the little girl, shaking her head violently.

'Horrible,' Anna said.

'I knew you'd think she was,' said Emma. The sprig of embroidered flowers was caked with custard, there was even custard in her hair. Anna burst out laughing.

'What's this?' she asked.

'I had a fight with her with the bunches,' Emma looked for the offending girl. 'She's gone home.'

'Who won?'

'Who'd you think?'

'You should see the other fellah,' said Ron. 'Not a splodge on her!'

Anna picked Emma up and carried her shoulder high out of the crèche. 'Victor ludorum,' she yelled. Ron would have laughed but he might have dropped the shopping, and Anna would not have been pleased about that.

Fleur was definitely not pleased. She was the old hand on Casualty yet it was she who had made the fool of herself while Jay was going about like the cat that got the cream. To top it all she had been 'invited' into Sister MacEwan's office for a 'chat', and by the look on the sister's face, they were not about to swap jokes. If only she hadn't made that slip-up this morning. 'Did you have a good night last night?' 'Yeah great!' Idiot!

Jean was finding it difficult.

'What time did you get to sleep last night?' she asked. Fleur shrugged, 'I don't know. Between three and four, I suppose.'

'I see. Do you do that often?'

'Depends on what you mean by often.' Fleur resented the interference in her private life. In her eyes it had nothing to do with it.

'You're looking tired.' Jean looked at Fleur's closed face, and sighed. 'I'm only trying to help you, Nurse Barrett.'

'Yeah. I know. I'm sorry.' Fleur leaned back in her chair and looked Jean in the eye. 'I'm sorry about what happened.'

'Yes, I realize that, but we must make sure it doesn't happen again, mustn't we? I've nothing against nurses going out and enjoying themselves. Sometimes it does you good to let your hair down but there are limits. You'll be knocking yourself up, girl!'

Fleur was looking at the floor. She knew it was true. Even then she could hardly suppress a yawn.

'It's your decision . . . you're old enough to be responsible for yourself, and I might add, in this job, for others too. People depend on you as a nurse. Today you made a mistake in personal relations, tomorrow it could be more serious. You can't keep burning the candle at both ends. You have to decide what's more important to you, your social life, or your work. But I'm warning you, another incident like that and I'll have no choice but to report you to the Director of Nurse Education.'

Fleur looked at the sister. She saw that she was serious, very serious. Suddenly Fleur felt cold and tired. She liked her job, prided herself on her work. After this evening she'd cut down on the night life, get her beauty sleep. She left the sister's office feeling like a chastened schoolgirl.

Mrs Carr felt much the same as she was wheeled on to the ward. She had promised Nurse Harper she'd co-operate. After all, it was in her own interests, because it *was* true, she wasn't well. She had to admit it. Such a sweet face the nurse had. Mrs Carr had put on her little girl voice and said, 'All right. I won't fight any more. I promise. I'll be good.' Nurse Harper had smiled. But when she saw the sister's face, as she stood waiting for her by the empty bed, her heart sank.

'You've been ordered bed rest,' she said. 'If you want anything you'll have to ask the nurse. You're not to stir from that bed.'

The auxiliary helped her into the bed in silence. She looked as though she wanted to be nice, but didn't dare. Mrs Carr sat bolt upright staring at the walls and past them to the blank October sky outside. She wondered whether the social worker would get Tristran's pills, and fretted as she imagined his face when he heard the key in the latch. His tail would wag . . . the whole of his rear end would go, as the door opened; then consternation! It wasn't her at all but some stranger. Poor Tristran. She would pick him up and cart him off next door where that Mrs Gardiner lived. He'd be frightened and that would set him off coughing. Oh dear! He was so sensitive. He knew very well that Mrs Gardiner didn't like him. He didn't need her to tell him.

She'd complained about his barking more than once. A terrible thought struck Mrs Carr . . . but she wouldn't, would she? Fear increased the pressure in her bladder. A sharp pain made her jump and brought the tears to her eyes. She was just about to throw the bedclothes back and go to the ladies' lavatory when she remembered. 'Bed rest.'

33

Oh dear. That meant calling for a nurse. She didn't want to be a nuisance; she'd get a reputation after the incident in the Casualty Room, but needs must . . .

'Nurse . . . Nurse!'

Beverley, caught between toileting Miss Hutchins and turning Mrs Nicholson, looked around for help.

'Nurse.' Mrs Carr's need was becoming urgent.

Beverley shouted desperately, 'Wait a minute,' shoved Miss Hutchins into the day room, and came to Mrs Carr's side. 'What is it?' she asked.

The genteel voice of the old lady lent dignity to her words, 'I want to spend a penny, Nurse.'

Beverley, harassed, ran off for a bed-pan and was told to walk by Nurse Bowell then, coming back with it, was told to be quick about it. Nurse Bowell was waiting for her to help turn Mrs Nicholson. The curtains were drawn and Mrs Carr sat at her convenience. Nothing happened. Beverley sighed audibly. Mrs Carr squeezed and a few drops tinkled painfully into the bowl. As Beverley took the pan to the sluice room Nurse Bowell called, 'Keep that for testing, Nurse.'

Beverley looked at the three drops in the bottom and raised her eyebrows.

Ron sat, nodding sympathetically in the gaps between Anna's sentences. He agreed with her of course. Our voices should be heard, there wasn't enough respect for the individual, they did get shoved around. How was she, Anna, ever supposed to learn about the clinical care of men on a surgical ward if she was pushed on to a female geriatric ward! Come to that, he was being shoved around too. He'd been moved from A. & E. under Charge Nurse Russell to Casualty, and he knew for a fact that Rose Butchins in the Nurses' Home had been lent to Male Orthopaedic.

'Would you like me to come out in sympathy?' he said.

'The union SHOULD do something about it,' Anna shouted. 'The sooner we're given proper student status, the better. Then they'll have to employ more qualified staff and stop relying on us for slave labour.'

'I see your point,' said Ron. 'But after all, nursing is essentially a practical profession. Theory in itself is not enough. We need the experience of working on the wards, and not just by being there as observers. You only learn by doing.'

'Doing what? Tying elastic round an old lady's leg.'

'Why not!'

Anna glared at him. He was infuriating. He always saw the other point of view; he'd never commit himself.

'I mean you're right in a way,' he said. There was a long silence.

'God, you're so bloody reasonable!' Her shout ended in an explosion of laughter.

Ron was relieved. 'Well, I'm glad it did you good. I find a freak out with a bit of heavy rock does the trick with me.'

'What do you mean?'

'Gets it out of the system . . . whatever it is . . .' Anna smiled. Anna was older than Ron, more experienced, had been married and had a child. She gave the impression of a woman who would not be denied. Who would dare? She could be frightening could Anna. He was surprised to find himself in her flat, drinking her coffee. There was a fury in her that was constantly demanding recognition. But now the fury was spent . . . temporarily. She looked sullen and sad. At least it made her more approachable.

'You're pretty fed up, aren't you?' he said.

Anna banged her mug on the floor. 'I'm fed up with being pushed about, I know that!'

'Why? Who else has been pushing you about?'

'Huh. Story of my life.'

Ron waited.

'First it was mum and dad ...'

'You know, I got the impression you were rather spoiled.' Anna gave him a warning spark. 'Well you seem pretty determined to get your own way.'

'I am now ...'

'I bet you had everything you wanted as a child.'

'I thought I did at the time!' Anna thought back to her mother and father, their cosy little life masking the misery between them, and their dreams, pinned on her. It was hard bearing the burden of other people's dreams, especially when their dreams don't agree.

'I thought I wanted to marry Keith ... but it was my mother. She wanted the kind of wedding for me that she would have liked for herself ... something to rival Princess Anne's you know?' Ron smiled. 'I was acting out her fantasy ... Happy Families ... and when Emma came along well, that completed the picture didn't it?'

'What about Keith?'

'You know why I married him? Because I had nothing better to do. Yes I did. He took my mother's place. He spoiled me rotten ... I admit it. Spoiling somebody's the most subtle way there is of pushing them around. Give them every little thing they want and they'll sink without trace into a meringue of a life. You'll not get a cheep out of them. You can do what you like with them.'

'So what happened?'

'I got bored.' Anna picked at the soles of her shoes like there was meringue stuck to them. 'I decided to live dangerously ...' Suddenly she laughed. 'I went home to mother.'

Ron giggled with her. He liked the way she could laugh at herself, it was as though her face opened and her soul popped out for a minute. 'After that?' he asked quietly.

Anna ignored the question and got up from the floor to

pour herself a drink . . . There was a bottle of cheap plonk on the table. Touching the bottle, she looked at Ron, but he shook his head. She poured one for herself anyway. 'You know, sometimes, I feel as though I'd been asleep all my life and I'd just woken up . . . It mightn't have been very pleasant sometimes, I mean it would be nice to believe in being "in love" for instance, and all that, but it's just illusion isn't it?' Her look challenged him.

Ron sighed. He felt put on the spot. 'Dreams are OK as an escape . . .'

'Yes, but not all the time.' Anna snapped back. 'The real world mightn't be very nice but at least it's real . . .'

Emma, sleeping off the effects of her encounter with the little girl in bunches, woke up and started to gurgle in the next room. Anna's face took on a pinched look but she ploughed on regardless. 'And I'm out in it, and living my own life the way I want it . . .' Emma's teddy hit the floor with a wallop. 'More or less,' Anna finished. She downed the glass of plonk and poured another.

'Then what are you getting so worked up about?' Ron asked. He knew it was a dangerous question, but he wanted to know all the same.

Anna looked at him, then turned away to the window, thinking. 'I don't know,' she said. 'Maybe I'm getting my own back.' She ventured a smile of apology. Ron was relieved she didn't know everything.

Emma pounced on her mother with a cry of, 'I'm awake now.'

'So I see, darling,' said her mother. Emma certainly had a way of making HER presence felt.

'If that woman calls for a bed-pan again,' said Beverley, storming into the sluice with an almost empty pan, 'I shall scream.'

Nurse Jarmolinski shook her head and smiled. 'It's all right my darling. Don't worry. You're doing fine.'

Beverley threw the pan into the sluice and leaned against it. 'You know I once knew a woman who put her clothes in there . . . she thought it was a washing machine.'

Beverley blinked. 'Never! You're having me on!'

'No. I'm not. It was her very best dress too . . . she was going to a dance . . . disco. It came out in ribbons . . .'

Beverley laughed and danced reggae style round the room. The auxiliary smiled. 'That's better. It's all right. I start to worry about them when they stop asking for bed-pans . . .'

Beverley looked at the nurse. Her warm eyes were twinkling at her. She knew more than Staff Nurse Bowell any day.

'Why?' she asked.

'It shows they've stopped caring . . .' Beverley frowned. '. . . whether they wet the bed or not . . . whether they live or not . . . whether we know they're there or not!'

'Some of them wet the bed anyway,' Beverley said after a minute's thought.

'Maybe, my darling. Maybe you and I did when we were little babies. We couldn't help it. Then we cried didn't we?'

Beverley nodded.

'And why did we cry? Because we didn't like it and neither do these old ones . . . but they can't help it either.'

'You like working on this ward, don't you?'

Nurse Jarmolinski smiled softly and tilted her head self-consciously. 'They could be your own mother couldn't they?' The thick Polish accent couldn't hide the emotion in the older woman's voice. 'So you put up with it when they pester you, eh, my darling?'

Rose, on loan to Male Orthopaedic, would not have agreed. Not that HER patients could ever be taken for her mother. Her mother was a hard nut but Rose would still have hesitated before comparing her with the lads with their legs in plaster. There was nothing wrong with them, that was the trouble. If they only felt ill they might be more docile. As it was, all they had to do was lie there and dream of action, or watch it second-hand on the telly. Rose, being on late shift, got the worst of it too, when the beer bottles came out. Then there was no holding them. Thank God they were well strung up. Norman Pollard with one leg suspended in midair was itching in more than just his foot. He watched the nurse's movements with bright eyes, a bottle of Newcastle Brown providing his only exercise. His right arm was strong enough to lift that little nurse right above his head he thought. He summoned her over. 'Hoy . . . Hoy, Nurse!'

Rose, weary from a morning's lie-in with no sleep thanks to her room-mate, Jay, and her fairy feet, and with a long evening ahead, trundled over to Norman's bed, hands on her hips.

'What now, buggerlugs?' she said.

Norman's face creased into a friendly smile and his eyes glistened. He changed the bottle from his right hand to the left. 'Can I give you a hand?' His hand caught her unawares in a sensitive spot.

'Gerroff!' she yelled. All eyes turned towards them and provided comic relief from the general boredom.

'Honestly, your mind's on one thing the whole time.'

'Yeah. Isn't it great?' Norman waggled his eyebrows but Rose was not amused.

'I've got better things to do than chase after you all day.'

'Sorry, Nurse. I'll not do it again.' His face was chubby and the cheeks swelled when he smiled.

The picture of boyish innocence. He put on an expression of contrition.

'Huh,' was Rose's only comment as she stalked off.

'Psst.' She looked back. He was gazing up at the ceiling

and whistling. Rose grated her teeth and her lips curled round a curse.

'Look at her snarl,' said Jack in the next bed.

'Aye,' Norman replied. 'She's the spittin' image o' that lion at the start of MGM Pictures.'

A crate of empties was stacked by the kitchen door. Rose chucked a couple more bottles in and looked at it with disgust.

'Home from bloody home,' she said.

Charge Nurse Stan Shilling raised an eyebrow. 'I see.'

'A crate of brown bottles standing at the back door ... All I need's the smell of burnin' paper as me mam forgets about yesterday's fish an' chips warmin' up in the oven.'

Stan laughed.

'It's not funny,' Rose snapped. 'Bunch o' thugs. They want a waitress not a nurse!'

'Hey!' Stan gave her a warning look. Rose bit her lip and straightened the bottles in the crate.

'That suit you better?' she asked.

Stan smiled sympathetically. 'Never mind, dear. *Match of the Day* tonight. They can let off steam a bit when that comes on.'

'Hoo-bloomin'-ray.'

'I don't know what you're complaining about. They think I'm a tart.'

Rose looked at his wide shoulders and frowned disbelievingly. 'What do you say to them?'

'Nothing. I learnt ju-jitsu in the RAF. So when I'm making the beds I give them a quick hold. Twist their arms. Know what I mean?'

'Will you teach me?' Rose grinned.

'All right.' Stan took her arm, bent her head forward,

touched the back of her knees with his foot and in no time at all she was on the floor.

'I said teach me,' she snapped. 'Not tie me in bloody knots!'

Beverley, almost at the end of her tether after her first day on G8, put on a plastic apron to take Martha Poole her tea.

'You've got to drink, love,' she shouted. 'Or you'll never get any better . . . Staff says so.'

Martha gave her one look and the hand struck out. The tea scalded Beverley's hand which shot in the air, upsetting the entire cup down the gap between her pinny and her dress. Anna, coming back on duty, heard the scream and rushed into the day room. She couldn't help a smile. 'This is where I came in,' she said.

Bev held the dress away from her skin and took off down the ward to the sluice room to towel herself dry, but Mrs Carr, seeing her coming, took the opportunity to call for her . . .

'I know . . .' said Beverley.

In the sluice room, she tore off the apron, and the dress slapped back against her chest. It felt like a cold clammy hand between her breasts. She shivered, reached for a bedpan and took it to Mrs Carr.

Nurse Bowell in passing said, 'I don't know why you don't leave the curtains shut all the time, Nurse. It hardly seems worth opening them does it?'

'Who is it?' Anna asked.

'New admission,' Nurse Bowell sighed. 'She's a pain.'

'What's wrong with her?'

'Urinary infection.'

Anna looked at the acting-sister. 'Why?' she asked. 'Why's she a pain?'

41

Nurse Bowell 'as in bow and arrow' shot her a dart from the eye. 'She must be in hell! Have you ever had it?'

'That's not the point, Nurse. Everyone else suffers in silence, why doesn't she?' Anna wanted to scream. As the curtains were drawn back she took a look at the old lady. Mrs Carr seeing the new face smiled at her, nodding her head for all she was in a carriage and four. Anna found herself smiling, and asking, 'And how are you feeling, Mrs ...' She looked at the name on the bottom of the bed ... 'Carr?'

Mrs Carr looked at her hopefully. 'Do you really want to know?' she said.

Beverley didn't bother to change her uniform again. It wasn't worth it. The shift was over. She trudged back to the Nurses' Home, the clammy hand intact. In her room, she changed into her jeans and jumper and took a look in the mirror. She tried to smile at herself, but it didn't cheer her up. She thought her teeth needed cleaning.

Jay reached her room moments later, flying up the stairs like Ginger Rogers in slow motion. Her view in the mirror had pink clouds in it and her teeth sparkled like Tony Curtis's. She pulled her eyes at the sides to make them slant and sucked in her cheeks. Tonight was a toss up between arterial infarction, reading a novel in bed and *Elvira Madigan* on again at Studio 2. *Elvira Madigan* won. If she hit the early show she could still read the novel in bed later ... although it seemed a pity to waste the use of the room when Rose wasn't in it. She could be so ... 'loud'.

Norman Pollard was just finding that out. Rose, summoned by a 'hey you' to Norman's side, was looking at him suspiciously.

'Where're you from?' he asked.

'Why?'

'Just makin' polite conversation.'

Rose stared at him stonily. 'You're a Geordie aren't you?'

'Whey hinny,' he said, putting it on a bit, 'how did you guess? Friendly lot, aren't we?'

'Well, I'm from Leeds and I don't feel friendly.'

'Whey that's a pity now . . . because I was just going to ask you to do me a favour like.' Rose waited . . . Norman shifted in the bed. 'It's me bum,' he explained. 'Well you don't want me to get bed sores, now do you?'

Rose looked at him then turned to Stan appealing for advice.

'Rub him, if that's what he wants . . . he's not been done for a bit.'

Norman was singing, 'In Leeheeheeds city . . . where the girls are so pretty . . .'

'Shurrup,' said Rose, as she reached for the cream. Norman raised himself obligingly and Rose started rubbing, gently.

'Oooooh!' Norman groaned. 'That's lovely . . . bit lower down eh?' Rose ignored him. 'By I've got a cheek, haven't I?' Norman looked at her. 'Get it . . .? Smile . . . smile, eh?'

Rose put the top back on the cream and Norman lowered himself again. She was just walking away when, 'Hey . . . pussy!' Rose turned furiously to him, not daring to speak.

'Get's the telephone, eh?'

'You've had it three times since I came on duty,' she hissed.

'Aye, well you know how it is . . . I like to keep me crumpet hot.'

Rose exploded. 'Well don't keep it hot at my fire,' she snapped. 'And if you dare to call me pussy just once more, I'll report you.'

Norman was on the point of asking, 'Who to?' but he thought better of it. She was upset. No doubt about it. He looked at her, dismayed. She hadn't finished yet. She was wagging her finger at him.

'I'm not a bit of a floozy in your local pub, you know. I'm a nurse, entitled to a bit of respect, and don't you forget it. I've got more important things on my mind than you, Mr Norman Pollard.'

Rose, in her present mood, or indeed in any mood might have made a better opponent for Bob Stetchley than Barry Hodgson. As he had promised himself he would, Bob wiped the floor with him. Squashed him flat against the squash court wall like a fly. Very satisfying! Or was it? There was still an uncomfortable itch in the back of Bob's mind. It was that fiver. It was Anna. Well, it was both. There was a lot at stake; his pride for one thing. Perhaps a more tentative approach? Keep up the left and dance round her a bit? He didn't usually bother with sparring. He was a bit rusty in that department. But he was still smarting from the last round. Perhaps if he put out one or two feelers, find out how she'd respond? Maybe put another bloke in the ring to try her out. Bob smiled. He looked across the changing room to the showers. Gerry Dent owed him a favour . . .

Chapter Four

It was Tuesday morning, Doctor Gould's round, and there was pandemonium on the ward. Staff Nurse Bowell, her mind firmly set on the sister's uniform (after all she WAS doing the job), and an automatic washing machine, had them running round like shop girls in the lunch hour. Everything had to be perfect, and on this ward it just wasn't possible. Every time you started a job something would happen and you'd have to leave it half done. The nurses seemed to end up doing three things at once all the time. A domestic was polishing the floor with a machine and every time a nurse had to cross the ward she had to jump over the lead, and they were in a hurry. Nurses didn't run but some had developed an interesting way of walking with bent knees, which, Mrs Carr thought, would have been an excellent technique for doing the tango. All in all, it was rather like watching formation dancers, all they wanted was frilly skirts. Certainly the middle of a ballroom floor was not the place to be reading a book. Mrs Carr sighed and put the book back on her locker. She couldn't settle. It was no use.

Beverley and the auxiliary were making beds. Mrs Carr watched them with interest. She noticed the plastic draw-sheets and the complaints as soiled sheets were dropped into the skip and fresh ones brought. So many of her fellow patients seemed incapable of holding themselves. It made her feel afraid. It wasn't popular with the nurses, she could see that, and she didn't want to be a nuisance. The familiar ache in her bladder suddenly became pressing. She was about to call when the staff nurse reappeared. She had been arranging flowers in the day room. She stopped at Mrs Nicholson's bed and looked at the notes.

'Mrs Nicholson hasn't been turned,' she said sharply.

The Jamaican girl gave her a look as she marched back to the office.

'Nurse!' Mrs Carr called. She shifted quietly feeling that somehow it would seem that she hadn't called at all and the nurse wouldn't mind. But she didn't hear, so Mrs Carr raised her voice. 'Nurse . . .'

Beverley threw a soiled sheet into the skip with wrinkled nose and trudged across to Mrs Carr's bed. 'We're busy,' she said. 'Can't you see?'

'Yes.' The answer was apologetic. 'But my need is urgent.'

Beverley sighed. 'It can't be, Mrs Carr. You only had one quarter of an hour ago.'

Mrs Carr felt most unpopular. She tried to explain. 'It's my condition, you see.'

Beverley went off to the sluice room, nursing a growing persecution mania as Anna emerged from doing the observations in the day room.

'Accident in the day room,' she said to the auxiliary as she passed her.

Nurse Jarmolinski left the bedmaking and went to the sluice room for the mop and bucket.

The thermometer was in Mrs Carr's mouth when Beverley returned with the bed-pan. She wasn't pleased to see Anna had got there before her. Anna looked at the pan and smiled. 'Well,' she said, 'there's nothing to stop us doing them both at once. Different ends.'

Dorothy Bowell frowned when she saw the curtains drawn round Mrs Carr's bed again and frowned again when she looked at Mrs Nicholson's notes and the old lady had still not been turned. The auxiliary was putting the mop and bucket back in the sluice room and was about to return to making beds when Staff called her in to help. The old lady groaned horribly as they turned her, and didn't seem impressed when Nurse Bowell shouted, 'It's for your own good . . .'

Mrs Carr heard it all through the curtains as she squeezed a few drops into the pan. It was agony to her, like passing sulphuric acid with bits of broken glass. Beverley who had never had the complaint but still had beds to make, tried not to look impatient, but snatched the pan away when Mrs Carr indicated she had finished, and marched off with a jerk of the head that said it had all been a complete waste of time. Mrs Carr lay back sadly, crossing her legs and Anna read the thermometer. The old lady looked rather low, she thought.

'Your temperature's coming down,' she said, smiling.

Mrs Carr, warming to her said, 'Oh, is it? I'm glad I'm good at something.'

The spark of humour made Anna look at Mrs Carr again. It had surprised her. Most of them just took what came without question, allowed themselves to be manipulated by their nurses, their faces blank and withdrawn.

Apart from Martha, when she was awake, and Granny Betts, who was only short-stay anyway, the day room could be more still and quiet than an empty room.

Nurse Bowell flew past calling, 'Nurse Newcross, haven't you finished observations yet?'

Anna pulled a face at Mrs Carr and passed on.

It was then that Mrs Carr felt a desperate urge to 'go' again. She gritted her teeth. She must wait a little while. She must try.

It was some time before Mrs Carr called again, and bad luck that the doctor's round was about to begin. She had met Dr Gould before, in Casualty. He was a charming man and he didn't mind. In fact when the acting-sister ignored the call it was he who beckoned to her and told her of the patient's need. Nurse Bowell smiled sweetly and thanked the doctor, then giving Mrs Carr a poisonous look, hurriedly fetched a nurse to attend to her. It was Nurse Slater, the Jamaican girl. Beverley felt embarrassed to be bringing the bed-pan during the doctor's round. She had never been on a ward during a round before, and somehow, him being a man, and a doctor, it didn't feel right. She felt that Mrs Carr was trying to draw attention to herself. Perhaps she thought the doctor would notice her and give her preferential treatment. In Beverley's eyes, Mrs Carr was being plain selfish and, though it wasn't her place to say so, her big black eyes let Mrs Carr know all the same.

'She thinks the whole world revolves around her!' she moaned to Anna as they went up to the canteen for coffee.

'Like my little girl,' Anna laughed. 'It's me, me, me all the time!'

Staff had threatened Beverley that she could help clean Mrs Nicholson's pressure sore so she had a lot to think about. She took her coffee to the sitting-room to prepare herself. She'd need a strong stomach. No bacon and eggs for her. She had seen that sore already and her stomach had turned then. Anna, on time for breakfast, waited in the queue. Barry Hodgson nudged Bob Stetchley and Bob turned to look. She looked more approachable this morning, somehow better humoured. Still, once bitten ... Gerry Dent was sitting at the next table.

'Now's your chance ...' He looked back at Anna, now head of the queue, 'There's the opposition.'

Gerry looked her up and down and shovelled his remaining beans on to his fork. He wasn't going to waste any. The woman behind the counter, remembering Anna from yesterday, put an egg and one rasher on to her plate then slid it on to the tray. Anna looked at the plate, looked at the

48

woman and put the plate back on to the counter without a word. They looked at each other for a second. Then the woman slipped another rasher on to the plate and with a barely perceptible nod of the head. Anna indicated that negotiations had been satisfactorily concluded. Both breathed a sigh of relief, tension broke, and Anna passed on to the check out. The crowd of technicians from the path. lab. were at their usual table, unmistakable by the layer of smoke that hung over it. Anna only half took it in, intent on her breakfast, and concentrated on finding herself a table where she could eat her precious breakfast in peace. It was usually the only meal of the day she *could* eat without interruption, for there was Emma to feed, to rescue, to suffer, or to help most other feeding times. Gerry Dent waited till she had settled, picked up his cup of coffee, and rose from the crowd of men. Bob gave him a sidelong glance as he moved off and tried hard not to watch as Gerry reached her table. He banged his knees together rhythmically, and took out his chewing gum. There was something about this whole business he didn't like. He was beginning to wish he'd made the move himself. Barry Hodgson was grinning at him.

'Oh, shurrup,' Bob said.

Barry shrugged and lit another cigarette. 'Want one?'

'No, thanks,' Bob snapped. 'I'm in training.'

The cup rattled on the table and Gerry Dent plunged into the seat opposite Anna. Anna looked up to see who it was then went on eating. Those were either nicotine stains on his hands or chemicals and if it was chemicals he worked in the path. labs.

'So this one drew the straw today,' she thought. Well she didn't think much of him, whoever he was. He looked like an idiot! Well so did Bob Stetchley come to that, but at least he didn't sit there twitching, looking as though he was going to burst out laughing any minute. He had a hollow chest too. All in all not a particularly fine specimen of manhood. He coughed.

'You shouldn't smoke,' she said. 'You'll get cancer.' His smile was awkward. He was puzzled. Anna eyed his fingers.

'Oh! No I don't smoke ... they're just ... stains ... I work in the path. lab.' Anna nodded. 'Ah,' she said, 'I thought I smelt a definite whiff of smoke about you.'

'Oh, that's Barry Hodgson.' He looked over to the table where he had been sitting. 'I work next to him ... smokes like a chimney!'

Anna, glancing over at the table, was just in time to see Bob Stetchley's head turn suddenly away. 'I see,' she said. Two staff nurses joined the table, prim as a pair of nuns, and delicately snapped into their crispbreads with their front teeth.

'Can I ask you a personal question?' Gerry was really grinning now.

Anna merely looked at him.

'Do you sleep with men?'

The two staff nurses crunched their biscuits loudly.

'I don't sleep with dogs.'

The crunching stopped. Anna and Gerry glanced at them, both at once, and the nurses moved as one, to another table. Anna's eyes sparkled with pleasure. 'I'm beginning to like you,' she said.

On the other side of the canteen, Bob caught their laughter, and hissed between his teeth. Anna, hoping like mad he was watching, reached out her hand to touch Gerry's arm and brought her face in close to his. 'Tell your friend ...' Her voice was like the vibrating beds in the solarium, it sent messages through his body. 'Tell your friend, if he wants to know the answer to that ... he should come and ask me himself.'

Gerry stared at her. He felt like a schoolboy come face

50

to face with Jane Fonda. 'All right,' he said, stepping sideways out of his seat and crashing into the table next to them. The two staff nurses looked askance and poured their tea back into their cups.

Anna was feeling excited when she got back to the ward. Beverley gave her a funny look as they washed their hands in the staff toilet, but she couldn't help smiling. She was playing the field. She'd not had the chance when she was younger. Keith saw to that. She'd missed out because of him. As soon as he'd seen her eyes start to rove he'd staked his claim, married her and that was that. Two months out of school. Well, she was making up for lost time, now. She was back in the game.

Dr Gould was still on his rounds, going from patient to patient sizing up individual needs. He shook his head at Mrs Nicholson. 'I think the very fact of her coming in here was enough for her,' he said, 'She resisted it for such a long time.'

Mrs Nicholson, deaf and ill, stared at him as at a total stranger. She had had a stroke then made a partial recovery, in spite of the complication of stiff joints thanks to her rheumatism, but her bronchitis had set in and worsened. She had pneumonia, and a drip hung by the side of her bed feeding her antibiotics. She never moved and on her admission was found to have a huge pressure sore. Dr Gould shook his head and left her to go into the day room. Nothing more he could do for her.

Mrs Lilley, sat side by side with her husband, was a different matter. His hypertension was improving and her diabetes was under control . . . only her feet to worry about now and they could go home. Mr and Mrs Lilley looked at each other. Their faces glowed. They could hardly believe the news.

'I'll see about getting you some special shoes,' the doctor shouted at her.

Mrs Lilley looked worried. 'Will they be expensive?'

Dr Gould smiled. 'They're free, dear.'

'Ooh!' Mrs Lilley was thrilled.

'You'll get your repairs done free, too.'

'An extra pair?'

Dr Gould and the sister exchanged a smile. 'Hope springs eternal,' they thought.

'No dear . . .' he shouted louder, 'you'll get your repairs done free as well.'

The whole of the day room heard with interest and mumbled about their not getting free repairs for their shoes.

'I'm not going home without him.' Mrs Lilley indicated her husband.

'No. Together. You'll go home together,' shouted Dr Gould. 'We'll have to get the social worker to come and see you to fix up your house for you . . .' Mrs and Mrs Lilley nodded but seemed only to be guessing at his meaning. 'Have things fitted . . . put the plugs where you can reach them, things like that.' Mrs Lilley nodded. Dr Gould smiled. He thought he had got through. He turned to Mrs Betts. 'Now then, Mrs Betts. Enjoying your holiday?'

'It's them as is supposed to be havin' the holiday.'

Dr Gould was patient.

'Yes but we want you to be happy too.'

Mrs Betts laughed. 'Ooh I am . . . it's like "Butlins" . . . my grand-daughter's a nurse.'

Dr Gould nodded. 'How's the eczema?'

'Better now . . .' she said, her tone indicating it had been terrible up to a mere second ago. 'That cream you gave me's helped a bit . . .'

'Good.' He was all for moving on.

52

'I don't want to be on my own you see,' Mrs Lilley insisted. Dr Gould nodded.

'I couldn't be on me own without him. We've been together for fifty years now.'

Dr Gould nodded. 'We'll do our best,' and got away at last. Martha Poole would not allow him to examine her and Miss Hutchins wanted to go to the toilet. Nurse Bowell sighed, opened the day-room door and called to Anna who was trying, without success, to help Mrs Carr find Radio Three on the head phones. Anna came, approached Miss Hutchins from behind and whisked her backwards in her wheelchair towards the door. Dr Gould frowned as Miss Hutchins' face expressed alarm at the suddenly receding world ... her hands spread in front of her as though she wanted to hold on to something. 'Nurse!'

Anna stopped and Miss Hutchins breathed a sigh of relief. Dr Gould approached Anna confidentially. He spoke kindly. 'How would you like it if someone suddenly came up behind you and wheeled you off without a word of warning?'

Anna blushed. 'Sorry.'

Dr Gould held the day-room doors for her as she man-oeuvred the chair. It made Miss Hutchins feel like a lady.

'I wonder if I could have a word with you about the day room, Sister.' Dr Gould spoke quietly, one hand on the door. 'I can't help thinking it's a little too tidy ... a little clinical ... I think it needs cheering up ... a few knick-knacks, pictures, china dogs and that sort of thing about the place might help. Scatter cushions!' He uttered the words as though they were a revelation. Nurse Bowell's face hardened and the doctor avoided her eye. 'Cleanliness is not always next to godliness, Sister. I think we must remember that. Make them feel at home. Stimulate their minds. They become institutionalized all too easily as it is.'

Anna smiled all the way to the toilet. 'He's right. He's dead right,' she shouted inside herself. 'She wants them to be like puppets just to make her job that little bit easier . . .'

She passed Beverley coming from the sluice room with a bed-pan.

'Why's it always me!' she demanded.

'Power to Mrs Carr,' Anna replied. Beverley stopped and looked at the student nurse. It was all very well for her. SHE didn't have to fetch the bed-pan every time. It wasn't HER the old lady was picking on.

Nurse Bowell was feeling pretty peeved when Dr Gould left the ward. She sat in the office, staring at a sheet of paper on which she had written 'scatter cushions, china dogs, stimulate their minds?' How on earth was she supposed to do that? Her fingers drummed on the desk, and when Beverley came in, almost in tears, complaining about Mrs Carr . . .! Nurse Bowell moved like a train and screeched to a halt by Mrs Carr's bed.

'I hear you wanted a bed-pan again, Mrs Carr?'

Mrs Carr was alarmed but didn't show it. 'That is perfectly correct.'

'When did this patient last have a bed-pan, Nurse?'

Beverley felt like the girl that grassed to the headmistress. 'Nearly half an hour ago,' she mumbled.

'Mrs Carr. My nurses have better things to do than run round after you all day. It's sheer selfishness. There are other patients on this ward. You should remember that. You should have emptied your bladder while you had the chance. You're a nuisance, that's what you are. A nuisance. Kindly stop pestering my nurses and behave yourself.'

Mrs Carr stared at the staff nurse, her eyes wide with astonishment. Beverley, looking back, saw them fill with tears. Slowly they dropped one by one, unchecked down the old lady's cheeks. She was a nuisance! A nuisance, that's all. Mrs Carr's hands lay heavily on the coverlet. She had not wanted to be a nuisance. She had not wanted to wet the bed like the other ladies. She was trying to be helpful. But what was the use? Slowly she looked round the ward. She would end up like them. She would end up just a body to be turned every two hours, another mouth to feed, a bladder to be emptied at their will. What was the point?

Nurse Jarmolinski drew the curtains round her. 'I brought you a bed-pan' she whispered. Mrs Carr let her help her on to the pan, performed, and slumped back in her bed afterwards without a word. Nurse Jarmolinski looked at her anxiously. 'How's your little dog?' she asked.

There was a long pause then a tremulous voice answered, 'I don't know.' Mrs Carr looked at the nurse beseechingly. 'No one has told me.'

Bob Stetchley looked for Anna in the canteen at lunch time but didn't see her. Gerry Dent had said he thought she fancied *him*! He was bowled over by her. 'Mustard,' he'd said. Well he'd better move in quick. 'Tell your friend to ask me himself.' Well if that wasn't a come on . . . Fleur Barrett was in the sitting room having her coffee. Bob approached her from behind and put his arms round her. The response was immediate.

'Hiya, raver,' he said, chewing on his gum.

Fleur gave him a wink. 'Hi, action man.'

'Listen. Will you do me a big, big favour?'

'Yeah.' Fleur's smile was expansive. 'Anything.'

Bob settled beside her and put his arm round her again. 'You know that first-year nurse . . . Newcross?' Fleur frowned. 'You know . . . pale face, Caucasian, hair, older than you . . .'

'Oh, yeah.'

'What ward's she on?'

Fleur shrugged. 'I think she's supposed to be on Male Surgical. Wait a minute, yeah. Ron's going out with her this afternoon and he's on a split. Yeah, so I suppose she is too.'

Bob didn't like the sound of 'Ron', and Fleur wasn't too used to acting as go-between for a bloke; she wasn't feeling on top of the world as it was.

Bob withdrew his arm. 'Thanks,' he said and wandered off absent-mindedly.

Ron was at the crèche before Anna, and Emma stood holding his hand waiting for Mummy like something out of Lucie Atwell.

'Don't be taken in,' Anna said. 'She's not usually like that.'

Emma glared at her mother.

'Where shall we go?' Ron asked her.

Emma swayed her body and coyly turned her toes in to each other. 'I like the swings,' she said in a persuasive little voice. Ron looked at Anna. Anna laughed.

'So do I,' she said. 'Come on, let's go and eat candy floss.'

'It'll ruin my teeth,' said Emma, self-righteously.

'Never mind, dear. You'll get some more.'

'*You* won't will you!'

'Yes, of course I will . . . free on the National Health.'

Ron and Anna swung Emma between them as they walked along to the park. She loved it and didn't want them to stop. And when Anna complained of aching arms she kept on and on until Anna rounded on her furiously.

'You selfish little sod. You wouldn't care if you pulled my arms out by the roots as long as you get your own way!'

Ron kept his silence as he walked alongside the two scowling women. He wondered which of them would give in and speak first. Suddenly Emma's voice sang out like pan pipes, 'you can get some more on the National Health,' she said. The sidelong smile she gave her mother took the sting out of the words, and Anna had to laugh.

'God. If you don't get your own way by stamping your feet you'll try something else . . .' She looked at her daughter. She was a source of constant amazement to her. 'You're a nuisance. Do you know that? A nuisance?' But the mood was broken and they were all smiling again.

Watching Emma on the swings, yelling at Ron, 'Push me . . . higher . . . higher . . .' her will dominating the young man's, driving him to do as she wanted, Anna was reminded of Mrs Carr. She was a nuisance all right, like Emma, but kill that vital spark that makes them a nuisance and they turn into cabbages or die. Dr Gould knew that. He goaded his old patients, irritated them, pushed them, made them resent him sometimes; and they were glad to get out, go home and live their own lives. Ron, exhausted, left Emma swinging aimlessly and watching him resentfully.

'Swing your feet,' shouted Anna. 'Do it yourself.'

Emma started to swing her legs and began to sway backwards and forwards again.

'Will she be all right on her own?' Ron looked at the little girl anxiously.

'Yes,' Anna watched her thrusting the swing in a wider arc.

'What if she falls off?'

Irritated, Anna glanced back at Ron. 'Then she'll learn to hold on tighter. She'll be all right.' Anna looked at Ron's worried face and sighed. She smiled at him reassuringly. 'You can't protect them all the time.'

He looked at her, he knew she was right but . . .

'She's all right. Really.'

Ron looked back at the child and laughed. 'She takes after her mother. The independent type.'

Anna couldn't quite make out whether his remark had

been a compliment or a criticism. For some reason, she minded which. 'Do you mind me being independent?' she asked.

Ron, heady with the spirit of adventure, decided to live dangerously. He smiled broadly at her, 'It's a challenge' he said.

Quick as a flash Anna retorted. 'I hope you'll rise to it.'

Ron was nonplussed. He tied himself in knots trying to work out whether she meant what he thought she meant and how to react to it. He'd had enough of living dangerously for the moment and changed the subject. She was going too fast for him. He thought about her life, her marriage, and now being alone. His face was serious as he asked, 'Do you manage all right, without a man?'

Anna laughed. 'For most things.' But seeing his face she turned away, thinking. 'It was hard at first' she said. 'It still is really. Especially with Emma. Sometimes I do wish there was someone I could turn to . . . I mean, my mother stayed with me at first, it helped with Emma but in a way she was just one more millstone round my neck.' Anna paused and kicked the grass at her feet. 'At least when you're on your own you can do what you like. Be yourself.'

'You can be yourself when you're with other people. You don't have to give that up.'

'No . . . if you know what yourself is.' Her face had a lost expression for a moment, so different from her usual determined look, a look that challenged all comers. Ron warmed to it. He wanted to put out his hand to her but he felt that she would suddenly laugh and he'd be left like an idiot. It was like offering bread to a woman who said she was starving then finding out she was on a diet. He restrained the impulse.

'Anyway you shouldn't get hooked on other people. They

have their own lives to lead and you have yours. I like being in sole charge.'

Ron thought of some of the down-and-outs he and his family dealt with in the Salvation Army Refuge. They didn't refuse the bread that was offered to them.

'Not everyone's capable of it,' he said.

Anna thought for a while about the old people on her ward. He was right and yet . . . 'People can do more than they realize if you let them . . . even if you have to push them . . . You know how most people seem to lose their identity when they come into hospital, they haven't got their things around them, among strangers, always being told what to do . . .' Ron nodded. 'There's an old girl on my ward, eighty-five. She's terrific. Well, she hasn't. She's a pain sometimes, she drives Sister mad, but only because she doesn't conform.'

'Yes . . . that's what makes me wonder sometimes about the Sally Army, you know, it's very tempting when you're helping people to change them at the same time . . . make them like yourself. I suppose you've got to help people the way THEY want to be helped.'

Anna thought for a while, her mind swaying back and forth with the movement of Emma's swing. In her imagination she saw Emma suddenly take off and swing herself high over the top of the rail and fall with a crash to the ground. She shuddered. 'But what if what they want isn't good for them,' she said. 'How'd you draw the line?'

Emma howled when she was taken from the swings, but Anna appeased her by buying candy floss. They stood outside the fun fair, each sweetening their own thoughts with the taste of pink fluffy candy, watching the big dipper from the safety of the firm ground.

Norman Pollard, lying in his bed with his leg in the air, had

59

a lot to think about too, and plenty of time to think it. He had bored the patients on each side of him as rigid as his plaster, going on about how sorry he was that he'd upset that little nurse and wasn't she a bit of all right and men were thick insensitive beasts and so on and so forth. Norman was really chewed up. He felt rotten. He remembered how her little legs had fetched and carried brown ale for him and he was grateful. He really was. Nurses were wonderful! He'd sent off for a T-shirt with the slogan *Give Nurses More* on it to prove it. He'd wear it in bed just to show her, only it hadn't come yet. There must be something he could do to prove how grateful he was for her services, and how sorry he was. She was a grand lass.

In the end his neighbour, Jack, said, 'Why don't you give me the cash and I'll totter off to the shop and buy her a box of chocolates.' Anything for a bit of peace.

Norman thought that was a great idea. 'Would the little lass be pleased?' he questioned.

'Yes, she would,' his neighbours reassured him.

So he reached into his locker, a difficult operation with your leg in the air, and got out his wallet. 'Make it a big one,' he said, handing over a fiver.

Jack raised his eyebrows but said nothing. He hobbled off down the ward on his way to the hospital shop, muttering, and shaking his head. 'That lad's makin' trouble for himself,' he said. But HE wasn't going to say anything. Oh no! HE wasn't going to start him off again, and he didn't want him going on all through the hospital request programme. Ethel had asked for a record for him specially. So, Norman lay back, quiet at last, having given Sister orders to alert that nice nurse from Leeds as soon as she came on, because he had something he wanted to tell her.

Chapter Five

When Rose came on to the ward late that afternoon, Charge Nurse Shilling passed on the message. 'Norman Pollard told Sister to tell me to tell you that he's got something to tell you so will you go and see him, Nurse.' Stan watched the steam rising and when it was almost coming out of her ears Rose took off at a smart pace for Norman's bed.

She stood at the foot of it, hands on hips and snapped, 'Now what? I'm telling you, Norman Pollard, I've had it up to here with you. You're a selfish, ignorant pig. That's what you are!'

Norman's neighbours looked on, amazed, as Norman pushed the box further towards the end of the bed ... Norman cleared his throat ... 'I er ... I'd like you to have this ... please,' he said, looking at Rose fearfully.

Rose glared at Norman, snatched up the box and tore off the paper. She looked at the box for some seconds, not daring to look up. Perhaps it was a trick box! There were dummy chocolates inside, or something? But it didn't look like that. A flush crept up her neck and landed on her cheeks. She burned with shame. She managed to look at Norman sitting on the bed, a little more hopeful now. He was just like a little boy, she thought. He didn't mean any real harm. His chubby cheeks trembled with apprehension, waiting for her reaction. No one had ever given Rose a posh box of chocolates before. It had a ribbon across it like the Queen wore ... Order of the Garter. Perhaps she was meant to share it with the other nurses? Suspiciously she checked Norman's face again. No. They were for her. All for her;

posh chocolates. A bloke had given her them. Rose Butchins, whom nobody liked, nobody had ever appreciated. Her face creased; she didn't deserve them. Oh, but she was going to have them all the same! Norman watched, dismayed, as the mouth quivered, the first sob came and Rose pelted down the ward into the sluice room.

'Oh heck,' he said. He was too embarrassed to look at either neighbour. 'Women!' he expostulated.

Jack shook his head and buried himself in his comic. That lad was makin' trouble for himself. But he wasn't going to tell him. Oh no! It was too late now.

Rose didn't dare look him in the eye when she came back on the ward and Norman didn't know whether he should call for her or not. So he suffered his itches and his sore bottom in silence. This wasn't what he'd planned. And he shuffled uncomfortably when Rose brought him his brown ale without even asking if he wanted any, and said, 'thanks,' as though she'd really had to screw up her courage just to get the word out. Then she'd run off before he could think of anything to say.

'Women!' thought Norman. 'Women!' He couldn't make head nor tail of them sometimes. It was an afterthought but it did cross his mind that he'd spent a whole fiver on her, when he knew very well the Dormobile needed new brake shoes. Women!

Bob Stetchley hadn't forgotten his fiver either, although it wasn't that, it was more the point of honour that worried him, and thinking about it, it wasn't that either. It was her. There was this Ron, and then Gerry fancied her too. He felt he was missing out and Anna became all the more desirable the more he thought about it. He'd sent in his sparring partner and she'd knocked him for six. She'd sent him an invitation but hadn't told him the date and time. She'd left him guessing. He itched to get it sorted out, get *her* sorted out, like a form that needed filling in; he wanted to pick her out of the in-tray, deal with her, then drop her in the out-tray; so he could forget about her, and get on with his life. The football season had started; he had more important things on his mind. That was it ... yes. She was trying to hook him for a more permanent kind of job than he had in mind. He'd have to watch it. That was the trouble with women. They wanted to be on your mind all the time, they never wanted to make way for other things. Bob chewed hard on his gum. If it hadn't been there he'd have scraped the enamel off his teeth. He tried to concentrate on the job in hand. He was testing urine for bugs, a boring job, a simple job, well beneath his capabilities. He had it in him to be a Pasteur; he'd strike out on a bit of his own research ... after the football season ...

Anna was surprised to find Mrs Carr lying with her eyes closed, slumped down in the bed when she got back to the ward. Perhaps she's tired, Anna thought. It was tiring, sitting there watching the nurses work ... a lot of patients said so. It was because they couldn't settle to anything. If they did they were always being disturbed.

Yes, it was tiring just lying there waiting for the nurses to punctuate your day with thermometers and cups of tea and going to the toilet and pills and bed making and so on and so forth. Anna picked up Mrs Carr's book. It had fallen on to the floor. *The Life of Sir Richard Burton* she read ... *The adventurer and explorer, the man of letters.* Anna smiled. She might get it out of the library herself some time. It sounded good. Nurse Bowell stood waiting to speak to her at the bottom of the bed. Anna rose and waited for the order.

'Help Nurse Slater would you, please? She's going to tackle Mrs Nicholson's pressure sore.'

Anna pulled a face as the sister turned her back to go. She'd seen that pressure sore the day before and a pretty sight it was. It smelt lovely too. Anna wrinkled her nose in anticipation. Mrs Nicholson had come in with the sore. 'Otherwise you'd never see anything like that on MY ward. Still, it's a challenge,' Nurse Bowell had said. Oh, well. All part of the job. Anna walked up to Mrs Nicholson's bed. The curtains were already drawn and Beverley was standing beside the prepared trolley, her hands in the air with the rubber gloves on.

'Right,' said Anna. 'What do you want me to do?'

'Me?' Beverley's eyes opened wide in horror.

'I've been told I'm to be your dirty nurse . . . you're dressing it, aren't you?' Anna looked at the huge eyes. 'What's the matter? You've learnt a bit about "a" septic techniques, haven't you?'

Beverley nodded hesitantly.

'And you saw Nurse Bowell doing it yesterday?'

'No,'

Anna frowned.

'I had me eyes closed,' said Beverley.

Anna stared then burst into laughter. 'You flaming idiot.' Beverley wasn't laughing. 'What have I got to do?'

Anna thought for a minute. It wasn't HER job to teach. Nurse Bowell should have made sure Beverley had taken it all in properly. She sighed. Well SHE wasn't going to do it. She'd just have to stand there and tell her as they went along.

'Heave ho,' she said and put her hands on the patient. 'Roll over towards me,' she shouted at Mrs Nicholson. 'We're going to do your dressing again.'

Mrs Nicholson groaned . . .

'Try and help, love,' Beverley shouted at her. 'It's for your own good.' And in her normal voice she added, 'I think.'

Nurse Jarmolinski came in to help hold the old lady, who,

64

although almost wasted away, was still heavy in the nurse's arms. They had to be careful not to trap the tubing from her drip and from her catheter, careful of trapping the old woman's arms underneath her and causing distress, careful of her stiff joints. It was hard work. Beverley, cleaning the wound, sweated from more than heat behind the mask she was forced to wear, and when it was all over and Mrs Nicholson lay back, in peace at last, it was quite a victory for her. She blew air up over her brow and took a deep breath.

'You'll make a nurse yet, my darling,' said the auxiliary.

Anna laughed. 'You know what I thought? I thought, I bet Mrs Carr asks for a bed-pan while we're doing this.'

Beverley avoided her eyes.

'She hasn't asked for one for ages,' Nurse Jarmolinski said. 'Has she asked you?'

Beverley shook her head and wheeled the trolley out of the way.

Anna and Nurse Jarmolinski looked at each other.

'Staff gave Mrs Carr a talking to ...' Nurse Jarmolinski whispered in Anna's ear. 'Nurse Slater thinks it was all her fault.'

'And was it?' Anna asked.

Going back down the ward, Anna glanced at Mrs Carr. Her eyes were open; she wasn't asleep after all. Anna hesitated, then passed on. She didn't like the look of that old lady at all.

Mrs Carr was still on Anna's mind as she left the ward and made for the crèche. It wasn't her place to question the sister, but she'd love to know what the cow had said to her. It was raining outside, October rain – dirty, dismal rain. Winter was coming. Anna was tired, Emma would be too, and a tired Emma was a fractious Emma. Still she should sleep. Anna looked forward to switching on the telly and switching off her mind. Her legs ached. She toyed with the idea of moving the television set into the bedroom. What decadence, to lie in bed with a milky drink in her special mug, watching the box, a hot-water bottle on her aching back. Marvellous. Sometimes being on your own was the best thing in the world. You could do just what you liked and you didn't have to talk to anybody if you didn't want to.

'Hi.' Just as she had passed Male Surgical, Bob Stetchley appeared out of the blue. Just passing by, no doubt. 'Just come off duty?' he asked, walking along with her.

'Yes,' she answered shortly. She was too tired for small talk. 'Have you?'

'No . . . finished hours ago. Left the squash racket in the locker.' He swiped the air with the racket and it made a sharp hissing sound, which made Anna blink. He grinned at her, chewing his gum. 'Fancy a drink?'

Anna sighed, 'No . . . thanks. I'm tired, and anyway I've got to go and fetch Emma.'

Bob raised his eyebrows, still grinning. 'Who?'

'Emma. My daughter,' Anna snapped.

'Ah.' There was a silence. Bob was thinking about it. 'Didn't see any wedding ring.' He swiped the air again with his racket.

'Stop doing that,' Anna frowned at him. He stopped. 'I'm divorced,' she said.

'Ah.' It was a different 'Ah' this time; a very satisfied 'Ah.'

'Would it make any difference?'

'Yes . . . no . . . yes. What?' said Bob.

'Or did you think my daughter was illegitimate?' Anna could have bitten off her tongue. It had sounded so prudish and bad-tempered.

Bob took a step backwards. 'Are you always so touchy?'

He was resisting a terrific urge to swipe the air again.

'I'm sorry.' Anna stopped and looked at him. She almost smiled. He liked it when she smiled. 'I'm tired.'

'Do you live near by?' he asked.

'Not far,' she said.

'Why don't I walk you home?'

Anna looked at him. Maybe he wasn't so bad after all. She thought she'd blown it with the talk about her daughter, and refusing to go for a drink.

'I have to collect Emma first,' she said.

'All right. Let's collect Emma.' He grinned at her and swiped the air with his racket. It set her teeth on edge, but she smiled.

Rose, on late, had locked the chocolates away in the office drawer. Her locker wasn't big enough. She would wrap the box in brown paper and smuggle it into the Nurses' Home, then she would hide it somewhere . . . where? On top of the wardrobe. Yes. No one would find it there. And tomorrow morning when Jay had gone, she would sit up in bed and eat the lot all by herself.

She didn't care if she was sick. They were hers, not to be shared! For once they were hers alone. Her rotten family were miles away in Leeds, they'd not get at them. Not on your life. What would she do with the box afterwards? Rose was planning ahead. She could do something proper like putting her tights in it all separate and neat like a lady. Rose began to smile and Charge Nurse Stan Shilling had the nerve to ask her if she's heard some really bad news, like her Mam'd died. Honestly. He'd laughed at her and expected her to snap back at him. But she didn't. 'There,' she thought. 'That showed him.' That showed Stan Shilling that his pupil, Nurse Rose Butchins, was the most unfathomable little person he had ever met. And he thought he'd actually just got to understand her. He shook his head. Well, he hadn't.

Emma was fractious, and tired. She demanded a carry home. Bob gritted his teeth and lifted her on to his shoulders. She woke up then; she felt very important up there and banged at Bob's shoulders with her fists. Anna didn't stop her. It was reassuring somehow. She thought of Mrs Carr. She rather wished she still had her fists out too. She didn't know why, but it was important to Anna. She couldn't get her off her mind. They hadn't spoken much on the walk home. At the door, Anna took Emma from Bob's shoulders and thanked him. It didn't occur to her to invite him in. Bob hovered for a moment. If she had said, 'Come on up,' he'd have been put off. But she didn't. She didn't seem to care whether he was there or not! 'All right then,' he thought. 'If that's what you want.'

Bob, leaving her at the door wished he'd asked her to arrange something for the next day, a drink at lunch-time maybe. Anna, closing the door behind her, was kicking herself for being too off-hand. He wouldn't try again. She sighed, and shook the rain from her cloak. It seemed a long time since she'd shared her bed with anything but a mug of Horlicks.

Fleur had been really fed up since her talk with Sister MacEwan. She was convinced her stars were going through a bad phase. Saturn must be in opposition to something or other. The moon making her unpredictable and tired, and influencing the attitudes of others towards her. But she was Leo, the sun, the life force. Her life-giving energy could outshine the lot of them. Her will would dominate. So Fleur told herself as she went off that night to the amateur theatre club. Fleur had taken up the club only recently, wanting to broaden her acquaintances. After all, nurses tended to come in contact with nothing but other nurses, doctors and hospital porters. What else was there? Now at the Theatre Club they got all sorts. The place was filled with wealthy young business executives who fancied themselves as actors and liked to give parties wearing well-used but expensive jeans, with fish and chips and champagne to wash it down. It was a marvellous atmosphere. A night at the club could be followed by drinking in the club bar, chatting with interesting people, mostly men, and then perhaps going on somewhere afterwards. Ray, a dissatisfied pet-food executive who wanted to be something in the UN, but was talented as an actor, was always glad to see her. She brightened up his melancholy. She was the gay life he'd always wanted and longed for from the dark shadows where he brooded on the fate that had made him a specialist in pet food. He didn't even like dogs. It would be a shame to deprive him of her rays of Leo sunshine just now. He needed her. And she fancied him. And there was his car . . . the smell of the leather on that new Porsche car! Thank God she'd got him to take the plastic covers off the seats at last. So what was the harm of going out for just one more night? She wasn't tired. It would do her good, relax her. She always felt better when she was relaxed and it followed that when you were relaxed you also did your job better. This was the persuasive reasoning that made Fleur offer her services after rehearsal . . . that is to help Ray go through his lines. He was very tense about the size of his part.

The evening stretched well into the early hours and under the influence of gin and Coke, an unusual combination which Ray had invented, he promised to take Fleur to the Pet-Food Ball. So that when Fleur hit the sack at last, she felt elated, rather than exhausted, and couldn't sleep for thinking up something original to wear; something that would serve for the ball proper with the old-fashioned band, the disco room and the jazz. There was going to be a jazz band too. So it had to be something adaptable, striking and very, very classy. Her mind tossed saffron silk and turned silver lamé till she was dizzy and on waking up the only conclusion she had reached was that it had to have a slit up at least one side.

Looking in the mirror, Fleur was glad she was black. If she wasn't she'd have looked very pale. She had reason to suspect that gin and Coke was not the best combination in the world. She checked her biorhythm chart before leaving the house. She was on a double low. Perhaps she shouldn't have gone out last night after all? Fleur shrugged. She had. That was that. The only thing to do now was to put a good face on the day and be thankful when it was over. Fleur was careful to get out in time for the bus. She would make a useful start if at least she was punctual on the job.

Anna too was punctual on the job, in spite of Emma. Emma had created when Anna had put a dirty dress on her. There was nothing clean left.

'Who'd you think you are anyway?' Anna had shouted at her. 'The Grand Duchess?' Anna's mother had said that to her when she was little and wouldn't put on her wellies. It made Anna laugh repeating it and Emma didn't understand why. So it was, 'Why, why, why,' all the way to the crèche and Anna was glad to deposit her daughter on Nurse Radley, in the hope that she would have changed the record by the time the afternoon came.

Nurse Bowell came on duty bearing mysterious parcels, which she left in the office. She looked like she had something up her sleeve and that made all the staff on the ward uneasy.

'What's she up to?' whispered Beverley as she and Anna made the beds.

'Search me,' Anna shrugged.

They were almost at Mrs Carr's bed. Mrs Carr lay in an embryonic position, as though asleep. But the eyelids fluttered, and when, now and again, she opened them, blank grey eyes stared out of the grey face. It turned Anna over inside. She remembered how she had felt when the excitement of leaving Keith had worn off. When the panic of being on her own began and the world seemed empty and alien and everything was beyond her. She had felt like giving up sometimes. Her face had looked soft and featureless, older too and the eyes were grey in expression if not in colour. Beverley and Anna approached her bed. She didn't move.

'Come on, Mrs Carr,' Beverley shouted. 'We've got to make your bed now.'

Still she didn't move. They went to her to help her sit up. She offered no resistance but she felt heavy as they swung her out of the bed on to the chair by the side of it, and when they threw the coverlet back . . . Anna and Beverley looked at each other in dismay.

'There's a sheepskin on, too,' Beverley said disgustedly. Sheepskins were used to help avoid pressure sores in patients on bed rest or who couldn't move properly. Anna glanced at Mrs Carr. She must have heard, but she made no sign that she had. She just sat, her thoughts bent inwards and no expression in her eyes.

'We'll have to tell Sister,' Beverley said. Anna nodded. She knew they would have to, but she didn't like it.

Nurse Bowell was looking through the returns from the path. lab. when Beverley went in. Mrs Carr's urine test had come up negative. There was nothing wrong with her. Nurse Bowell was not surprised. She'd suspected that old lady all

71

along. Then when Beverley came in and told her ... she pursed her lips.

'Very well. If that's the way she wants it,' she said. She made out a new card for the Incontinence Kardex system, writing 'Anne Carr' in bold letters across the top, and instructed Beverley to remove the sheepskin. She would have to have an air bed, and plastic sheets, and to start with, at least, paper linen would have to do. Paper sheets got hot and creased. Bed-ridden patients didn't like it.

'There's nothing wrong with her,' said Dorothy Bowell, 'Dr Choudry will have her up and about when he finds out.' So the bed linen was changed and Mrs Carr returned to it and tucked in, leaning back against the pillows with her eyes closed, and her book plonked before her unopened. Nurse Bowell decided to pay her a visit.

'There's nothing wrong with you,' she explained.

Mrs Carr heard the words. She didn't care. Even the burning in her bladder had stopped mattering. It seemed farther away somehow. Only she felt so hot. Her head felt hot. She opened her eyes and the sharp lines of the staff nurse's face were, thankfully, blurred.

'It's all imagination,' she was saying, 'and I'm warning you, it's in your own hands. If you don't make an effort to control your motions, we'll have no choice but to fit you with a catheter.' Nurse Bowell waited for a reaction. Mrs Carr let her head fall to one side and she muttered quietly, 'Do what you like.'

Nurse Bowell felt a moment of surprise, but did not follow it up.

'I don't care.' Mrs Carr finished. The staff nurse raised her eyebrows, took a deep breath and went back to the office.

Anna, doing the observations, noticed the temperature rising. It was being checked two-hourly and had risen one degree since first thing that morning. It didn't make sense. Dr Choudry, learning of the negative result, asked for another test, and did not prescribe antibiotics. If the next test was negative, then maybe there WAS nothing wrong with the old lady after all, not in his department anyway. It would be a case for Dr Gould, the geriatrician, and perhaps the psychiatrists.

Anna was concerned, but it was busy on the ward that morning. Mrs Lilley had gone off with the social worker to look round her house. They were going to see what needed doing to it so that she and Bert could go home again. She had been so excited that she'd made the nurses get her ready an hour and a half before she was due to leave, then sat in the day room fretting and continually asking what time it was till the social worker arrived.

Martha Poole had soaked Beverley again, but with orange squash for a change.

'Why is it always me?' Beverley muttered for the umpteenth time.

Mrs Betts decided to have a sing-song all to herself to liven the atmosphere when Sister made them switch off the telly. Mrs Betts had been watching *Digame*, the Spanish programme for beginners, and resented its loss bitterly. The rest of the residents looked less than impressed when she squawked, 'Here we are again, happy as can be . . .' Nurse Bowell had the answer to Dr Gould's request to stimulate the patients' minds. She had the porters bring a blackboard and coloured chalks. Then she wrote on it the day, date, and season in different colours in huge letters and put it in the day room. The old ladies looked at it with interest.

'What day is is?' she shouted.

Blank faces stared back at her.

She repeated the question. 'Martha . . . can you tell me what day it is?'

Martha woke up suddenly and Staff repeated the question yet again. Martha paused and glowered at Nurse Bowell, then she sat back in her chair. 'Haven't got me glasses on, ye silly bugger.'

Unperturbed, Dorothy Bowell pressed on, silencing Granny Betts who was always chirping up, trying to goad the others into action, into thinking. She made them look out of the window to see what the weather was doing, and only succeeded in fretting Mrs Lilley who hadn't got her winter boots with her and was afraid of the walk up the garden path from the mini bus. It would take her a long time walking at her pace! After that Nurse Bowell opened her mysterious parcels.

'Oh, them's nice,' said Nurse Jarmolinski, eyeing the ducks that would adorn the day-room walls.

Anna sighed as she banged in the nails. 'Hardly nursing duties,' she muttered. Still, it passed the day on and there was no sign of her getting sent back to Male Surgical where she was supposed to be. Sticking ducks on the wall was no more incongruous to her teaching programme than making garters, or toileting Miss Hutchins. She banged a nail in, thinking of Nurse Bowell and found satisfaction in it.

But Jay was learning. Fleur was teaching her dressings. They didn't learn that in the school, after all it was a practical skill which they could learn on the job in Casualty. Fleur quite liked teaching and Jay didn't ask too many questions she couldn't answer. They had a patient with a wound on the head in the treatment room. She'd banged it against the light switch when she'd stood up after picking up the remains of the teapot she had dropped. Fleur reflected on biorhythms and considered it more than likely that the poor woman was also on a double critical day.

'It would be interesting,' she said, 'to make a survey of all the patients that come into Casualty. We would if we were in Japan.'

Jay looked up, puzzled.

'Check their biorhythms ... see how many had accidents on critical days!'

Jay watched Fleur cleaning the wound, thought for a minute then asked, 'What's a biorhythm?'

'Don't you know?' Jay shook her head, 'I thought everybody knew about biorhythms.'

She waited for Jay to ask her again, but she didn't. Jay didn't want to show her ignorance. She thought it must be part of the course, perhaps a lecture she had missed.

'Do you want me to tell you?' Fleur said at last.

'Yes,' said the patient.

'Well ...' Fleur was enjoying herself now, clearing the hair from round the wound with a razor. 'It's all right dear, I'll leave you some,' she said to the worried woman. 'There's three different rhythm cycles, you see. Physical, that's twenty-three days long, emotional, that's twenty-eight days long and intellectual, thirty-three days. Each cycle has a peak and a trough.' The razor described the graph in the air before descending once more to the patient's head. 'Now about six times every year, two of the cycles reach a peak or a trough together. If they coincide on a trough, that's known as a double critical day. But once a year, all three coincide and that's when you're really in trouble.'

Jay was still wondering if it was part of the course. It sounded rather confusing and she was having enough trouble trying to sort out the circulation and what happened in cardiac arrest. She'd been looking at it last night, but couldn't really understand what systolic and diastolic pressure meant. She could take blood pressures all right. But what did it all mean? And now there was all this biorhythm stuff. Jay sighed. 'I'll never pass the exams,' she said.

'Oh it's nothing to do with nursing.' Fleur reassured her. 'Mind you, I think it should be! Everyone should have their biorhythm chart done. I have.' Fleur paused and looked at the wound. 'I think this is just an abrasion, you know'. Jay looked and nodded. 'No stitches dear.' She smiled at the patient. 'Now take me, according to my chart I shouldn't even have left the house this morning. Something terrible's bound to happen.'

'Does it really work?' Jay wrinkled her nose in disbelief. If it wasn't part of the course it was probably nonsense anyway.

'Of course it does,' Fleur looked irritated. 'The Japanese run their taxi companies on biorhythms. On certain days of the year, they won't let their drivers anywhere near a company car.'

Jay giggled, 'I thought that was just women!' she said. But the smile faded as Fleur turned on the full power of a withering glance. Backing away, Jay went to fetch Sister to check the wound.

Sister MacEwan agreed with her student. The wound did not require stitching. She smiled at Fleur, she was behaving herself today, hadn't put a foot wrong since she'd spoken to her. Jean was pleased. She liked Fleur. She was a good nurse. It would have been a pity to have to report her to the powers that be. It could have a bad effect on her future career. And Fleur was trying very hard in spite of the circumstances. She found Jay irritating. Fleur was always joking and Jay had no sense of humour, no sense of the ridiculous. It was because she was a Virgo. They were so pedantic! There was nothing more annoying than someone who, instead of laughing, questioned the validity of your jokes. Still, Fleur was bearing up, and Sister was softening towards her again. It was going to be all right. She might get through her double critical day yet.

Jay caught Sister before she went out,

'Have you heard how that old lady's getting on?' she asked.

Jean looked blank. 'What old lady?'

'That Mrs Carr. Came in with urinary infection.'

'Oh!' Jean remembered and was sad that she had forgotten her so soon. 'Out of sight, out of mind, I suppose,' she said. 'I don't know,' she sighed. 'That's the trouble with Casualty. You never get a chance to follow a case through. We pick up the pieces and somebody else puts them together again. Pity really.' It was more than a pity. It was plain unsatisfying. She too wondered about Mrs Carr. She had been an unusual old lady, and she felt somehow responsible for the bad time she'd had in her department. She hesitated, her hand on the telephone in the office. Surely it could do no harm just to ask ... Jean picked up the phone and dialled the number of Ward G8.

Nurse Bowell answered. The acting sister was usually in the office, preferring paperwork to the dirty work on the ward. She was, at the time, deeply immersed in choosing the make of the automatic washing-machine she wanted, while her students and the auxiliary saw to the toileting. That's what they were there for after all. Jean's voice was apologetic.

'I just wondered how she was ... we never seem to find out what happens to patients once they leave here ...'

Nurse Bowell was very charming. Her charm would have broken a bottle at three paces. 'She's all right, apart from making a damned nuisance of herself all the time ... Her urine test showed negative.'

That sounded odd to the Casualty Sister. Nurse Harper had got a positive reading doing a spot check. Still, it wasn't her place to question. 'I think she's probably the type that makes a fuss for the fun of it.' Nurse Bowell underlined a

77

top loader of a foreign make in red, and considered its price.

Jean apologized for bothering her, 'I know how busy it can be on your ward . . .'

'Quite all right, Sister. Any time at all. Oh, and thank you so much for warning us about Mrs Carr. It's nice to know when a prospective trouble-maker is on the way . . .'

Jean put down the phone and sighed. That wasn't what she'd meant at all.

Nurse Bowell snorted. 'What's it got to do with HER anyway?' she muttered.

Mrs Carr had to be changed twice that morning, and neither time had the old lady asked for a bed-pan. If she had been a nuisance before, she was more of a nuisance now and a source of growing concern to Anna and Beverley. Beverley felt guilty. She felt that somehow it was all her fault. Anna blamed her too. Beverley could feel the aggro coming over to her from the student on behalf of Mrs Carr. But deep down Anna knew it wasn't Beverley's fault. It was Sister's. She should have seen to it that her pupil nurse was not put under too much pressure on her first ward. She should have understood, and sympathized more with the old lady's needs. It was her fault. That bitch! Well she would try and get to the bottom of it somehow. Anna couldn't stand by and watch the old lady just being destroyed. It was as though Mrs Carr was part of herself . . . her future. They were both on their own and determined to make the best of it. If Mrs Carr could be destroyed, then so could she. Mrs Carr's condition touched her personally. 'It's the individual against fascism,' Anna told herself. 'Yes, that's what that Nurse "Bowel" was.' Anna used the word Bowel with satisfaction. The name suited her. She was a fascist.

Anna looked at the old lady lying there so apathetically.

'It's you and me against the world, love,' she thought. 'And we're going to win.'

Jean felt restless. Her call up to the ward had worried her. She couldn't do right for doing wrong just now. She'd meant to do Mrs Carr a favour by preparing the sister. She'd meant the sister to treat her carefully, gently. And all she'd done was to set the sister against her. How did a woman like Nurse Bowell get to be a nurse? Where did her training fail her? Because fail it must have done somewhere. Nurse training demanded more than just teaching girls how to bandage a foot! It demanded teaching an attitude. An attitude of caring and understanding. Nurse Bowell was no ministering angel!

Fleur breathed a sigh of relief. She was doing very well. She'd got to lunchtime and nothing had gone wrong. Well, she'd made a mistake but Sister hadn't really minded. They'd had feet all morning, sprains, cuts, abrasions, hammer toes and fractures. They'd had the lot. Then this young lad came in with a limp. What was she supposed to think? He wasn't there when she saw the doctor and Sister had told Fleur to examine the lad, see what she could find. He had seemed surprised when she'd made him take off his shoe and sock, but he hadn't said anything. Then Sister came in and asked her what she was doing? It seemed he'd got something in his eye. Fleur had held her breath for a moment, but Sister MacEwan was a good sort and she'd just laughed. So had the man and Fleur joined in. She didn't mind a laugh at her own expense. Why should she? It was all good fun. So Fleur had relaxed, let up the watch on her tired, raw nerve ends. Everyone had heard about it. Ron, when he saw her coming, put one hand over his eye and limped, shouting, 'Aye, aye, Jim lad.' Even Jay had seen the funny side of it. That Stiff Nurse Harper.

'Tut tut,' Ron joked. 'What HAS got into Nurse Barrett?'

'She must be on a double critical day!' Jay said. They were still laughing.

Fleur defended herself, 'Anyone can make a mistake,' she said. She'd never seen Jay smiling so much. She was really letting her hair down. Good for her!

'As long as you don't make any mistakes with your boyfriends,' Jay teased her. 'Or do you use the biorhythm method.'

If Ron had laughed it might have been all right, but he didn't understand the joke. He and Fleur looked at Jay, tears running down her face, elated by the unusual event of having cracked a joke. It was like a flash of lightning. Fleur hadn't even felt it coming. She heard herself shouting, 'Who the hell do you think you are, insulting me? I'm not some cheap tart!' Ron tried to calm her down, but she shook his hand from her arm. 'You're an ignorant little bitch!' Jay's face stopped Fleur in her tracks; immediately she was sorry. Jay's face was quivering. She'd come out of her shell and got stamped on. It would be a while before she came out again. She'd blown it, really blown it. Sister MacEwan faced her with a troubled expression. Looking into her eyes, Fleur knew that there was nothing for it now. Sister MacEwan would have to report her to the Director of Nurse Education. She was for the high jump.

Chapter Six

In the Nurses' Home, Rose, behind her locked bedroom door, reached up for the box of chocolates. She had had no breakfast. She tore off the cellophane and arranged the blue ribbon across the dressing-table mirror. It made her think of those sashes beauty queens wore. Her face wouldn't win beauty contests, she knew that. But so what? She was Rose Butchins. She mattered, and somebody else actually seemed to think so too.

Rose smiled at her reflection and sighed. She went back to bed and lost herself in a world of hazelnut whirls and praline cracknel. She liked the soft centres best, but she always saved them till last. She lay back, sighing with pleasure and contemplated the joys to come. By lunchtime she would have worked her way through the hard nutty ones and abandoned herself to the melting flavours of the strawberry creams, and all because of Norman Pollard; delicious Norman Pollard.

Norman lay steaming in his hospital bed. Sweat poured from his brow. He had a nasty feeling that that canny little nurse from Leeds had gone sweet on him.

'Whey,' he consoled himself, 'I'll be out soon. Then she'll forget all about's. I'll get back to me usual crumpet and she'll get her mind back on her job. Why aye. It'll be all right.' But he wasn't so sure when he saw Rose's face that day. There was something different about her. He couldn't quite say what . . .

'Hey Jack,' he called, 'what's different about Nurse Butchins eh?'

Jack thought it was a game like 'I Spy'. They did all sorts to pass the time. 'I don't know . . . has she changed her hair-do?'

'No!' Norman lay back and watched as she walked Tammy Philips to the bog. No . . . it was something far worse than that. She'd gone all soft. You only had to look at her face. Norman's heart sank. Rose, feeling his eyes on her, looked across to his bed and smiled a gentle, sweet smile. Norman thought her jaw would crack. He had a mental picture of her with her jaw bandaged up, looking miserable and immediately dispelled it again, accusing himself of being the mean rotten bastard *she'd* accused him of in the first place.

He smiled back hesitantly. A pink flush brightened the colour of Rose's cheeks. 'Hey,' Norman thought. 'Perhaps that's it. She's not half looking peaky. That soft look might just be a bad stomach or something.' Reassured, Norman relaxed and started going through the maps he'd had brought in to plan his trip round Kent. That's what he was going to do when he got out . . . all on his own, take the Dormobile round Kent, getting up when he liked, going to bed when he liked, eating what he fancied, when he fancied it. Great! That was the life. Fancy free! He had some days off before he went back to work. That's what he was going to do. He'd thought of taking Suzy, his current crumpet, but women always had you on the go, chasing round the countryside looking for a ladies' loo. He'd see her later . . . when he got back. Fancy free, eh? Great!

Suddenly Rose dropped Tammy Philips and made a dash for it. The men all watched with interest as she bolted for the staff toilet. Norman nodded. Her hand was covering her mouth. That was it. Bad stomach. He'd been right. Poor cow. He settled back into his maps deciding he'd be extra nice to Nurse Butchins today because she was 'feelin' a bit delicate like'. He was deep in an argument with himself over whether he should take the 249 off the M20 or try the 628, which looked more interesting if the engine would make it up the hill, when he heard someone say, 'Planning a trip?' He looked up and found Nurse Butchins smiling at him. He remembered she wasn't well. She still looked pasty.

'Aye,' he grunted.

'Oh.'

'Feelin' better?' he asked.

'Yeah,' she answered.

'Oh,' he said. 'You want to get out a bit . . . get a bit of air . . . put some colour in your cheeks.'

'Yeah,' said Rose, looking at the map. 'Where are you going? To the seaside?'

'Well, I might take it in, like . . . on me way.'

'Oh, lovely.' Her face looked so touching, so pale. The poor lass obviously wasn't well.

'When are you going?' she asked.

'Friday,' Norman said. 'First thing.' That'd put her off. Women didn't like gettin' up early.

'Great,' she said.

'I'm going in me Dormobile,' he added. 'That's if I can get new brake shoes fitted in time.' He thought of the fiver with regret. 'It's a bit rough like, pretty clapped out . . . no curtains at the windows.'

She was smiling.

Norman tried harder. 'And I don't like camp sites proper. Not very much anyway . . . so there'll be no facilities . . . just park it in a field when I feel tired like, and kip there and then.'

Rose was still smiling. She wasn't saying anything but somehow she was managing to break him down little by little . . .

'Still, I expect you'll be workin' . . . or I'd have asked you

83

to come with 's,' he said, feeling pretty sure that that had finally put her off.

'I'm off Friday,' she said, 'and Saturday.'

'Oh.' How could you say, 'No'. To Norman it would be like kicking a dog after it'd licked you. He couldn't bring himself to do it. 'Great,' he said, with less conviction.

'Will you pick me up?' Rose asked. 'I'm in the Nurses' Home.'

'Certainly.' Norman promised.

In the next bed, Jack shook his head. That lad was askin' for trouble ... no doubt about it. Rose, taking a bed-pan to the sluice, dreamt of cows and green grass and trees and real fresh air. She was walking on pink clouds. Norman couldn't figure it out. How had it happened? How HAD it happened? He'd not any intention of asking her. It was a mystery to him. A real mystery.

Anna had done a lot of thinking in her break and when she came back on shift late that afternoon she had decided to act. But not just yet. She would wait till the 'Bowel' woman went off duty, in an hour's time. She would wait till the acting sister had snapped the Kardex shut, and putting on her cloak she snapped shut that part of her mind that dealt with the ward and all the people on it. No chance of HER sleep being disturbed through worrying over her patients. Nurse Jarmolinski and Nurse Slater left with her and the late shift took over. Everything felt less pressurized in the evening.

Most of the old folk were back in bed, and tired after their spell in the day room. They had more time to spend on those that needed that extra bit of attention. Anna took Mrs Carr a cup of tea. It wasn't tea time, but Staff had said, 'Yes ... if it'll cheer her up.' And Anna made the tea, weak, as Mrs Carr liked it, pouring it into one of the china cups usually kept for the doctor, after his round.

Mrs Carr, hearing the tinkle of teaspoon against best china, opened her eyes.

'I've brought you a cup of tea,' Anna said. 'I noticed you didn't drink yours at teatime.'

'It was the taste . . . all tannin,' Mrs Carr explained. 'I get mine nearly last and by then it's over-brewed in the pot.'

Anna nodded, laid the tea on the locker and helped Mrs Carr to sit up. The old lady eyed the cup and saucer. 'I'll be getting you into trouble,' she said.

Anna smiled and put the cup and saucer into her hands. 'Nurse Bowell's gone off.'

'She doesn't like me, you know,' Mrs Carr said plaintively.

Anna sat in the chair by the bed. 'I think you're marvellous,' she said, with an emphatic nod of the head.

'Do you really?' Mrs Carr was only too ready to believe it.

'Of course I do. You're so independent. I only wish I could believe I'd be like you when I'm your age.'

Mrs Carr smiled. She was pleased. The tea tasted better out of china. Those thick pots spoiled the taste so . . . really tea on the ward was usually quite undrinkable.

'Did you used to work?' Anna asked.

'Oh yes . . .' Mrs Carr was warming up now. 'I had to . . . James was handicapped you know, wounded in the war . . . the first one of course. The trouble is I was never any good at anything.' Her face, looking over the teacup, asked for denial.

'I can't believe that,' said Anna, right on cue.

'Well, I WAS good at sewing,' Mrs Carr sighed, remembering her days as a seamstress in the sweat-shop behind the tailor's. 'But I was always too much of a perfectionist, you see. It meant I took far too long over everything and never got through the work in time, so I had to finish off at home. I used to work very long hours and it was poorly rewarded, you know.'

Anna nodded.

There was a pause while Mrs Carr cast her mind back over the possibilities of her past life. 'And then I could sing,' she said enthusiastically. 'I had the voice for opera. I was told that!'

Anna was amazed. Her face showed it.

'But you see I have no sense of pitch.' Mrs Carr went on, 'Life can be very frustrating can't it?'

Anna thought for a moment, puzzled. What on earth was she to say to that? 'Yes,' she answered after a moment. It seemed the most likely reply.

'I sing to Tristan sometimes,' Mrs Carr's face assumed a melancholy expression. 'His voice is almost as good as mine now.' A wistful smile illuminated her face.

Anna was touched. She didn't know why. Her mental image of the old lady and the dog, singing together, was ridiculous, yet touching. The dog meant such a lot to her. He was her only companion ... the only one left to listen to her singing.

'How is Tristan?' Anna asked quietly. She was alarmed to see the cup shake in the saucer. Anna rose and took it from her, holding the trembling hand.

Mrs Carr reached for a handkerchief and wiped her eyes. 'I don't know,' she said.

'Didn't you ask the social worker, Mrs Carr? When she was in seeing Mrs Lilley about her shoes?'

'I didn't want to be a nuisance.' The words cut through Anna like a knife. A mixture of fury and pity fought inside her. She hadn't wanted to be a 'nuisance'. But the old lady was still talking ... Anna had got her started and now she was glad, very glad to get her worries off her chest.

'You see my neighbour's looking after him ... Mrs

86

Gardiner. She doesn't like dogs. She complains when Tristan barks, and he can't help it sometimes you know . . .'

Anna nodded.

'Consequently, we don't get on,' Mrs Carr sobbed. 'Tristan must have his pills regularly, he has a heart murmur, you see . . .' The words were squeezed out of a throat aching with suppressed tears, 'I'm afraid she won't give him them at the proper times . . .'

Anna squeezed her hand, sitting on the bed now, doing her best to comfort her. 'Oh, surely, she will . . .' she said.

But Mrs Carr's voice drew strength from her feelings of resentment. 'You don't know! She can be most vindictive.'

Anna said nothing, but looked into the despairing face of the old lady.

'Oh dear, I'm sure she's let him die and they're afraid to tell me.'

It was like a flash of lightning to Anna. That was it! That was the lifeline she could throw to Mrs Carr!

'I'm sure she hasn't.'

Mrs Carr was sobbing quietly, feeling a little ashamed of herself. 'You think I'm just a silly old woman, don't you?'

'No.' Anna's voice was warm, reassuring. There was no trace of the usual edge. She had no axe to grind here. She put her arm round Mrs Carr and the old lady let her head rest on the nurse's shoulder.

'He's all I've got you see. I'd discharge myself from the hospital.'

Anna looked disapproving.

'I would! They tell me there's nothing wrong with me. But I don't want to be a nuisance. I know I have to be a good girl and do as I'm told.' Anna rocked her gently. 'And I feel so weak anyway . . . my legs wobble when I try to walk.'

Anna's head dropped down over the old lady's face, her cheek on her brow. She frowned and raised her hand to feel

87

the forehead. It was burning. Why had she not complained? Because she didn't want to be a nuisance? There was something wrong with that path. lab. report. Anna was sure of it. She reached for the thermometer, put it in Mrs Carr's mouth and felt her pulse.

'Your temperature's gone up again' she said to her. 'Why didn't you say you were feeling poorly?'

'I don't know.' Mrs Carr said 'I don't care any more.'

'You mustn't lose heart.' Mrs Carr was crying again. 'You want to get better for Tristan, don't you?'

'He'll have forgotten me ... or died ...' The old lady would not be comforted.

'I'm sure he hasn't,' Anna insisted.

'Do you think so?' Mrs Carr looked at Anna, the grey eyes, wet with tears, beseeching the nurse to say it wasn't true; her Tristan was still alive, still loved her best in the whole world ... Anna vowed that somehow she would prove it to the old lady.

'I'm sure,' was all she said.

Mrs Carr felt better for a good cry, finished her tea and used a bed-pan. She only hoped that 'they' wouldn't think she was just being a nuisance again, creating a fuss. But Nurse Newcross didn't seem to think she was. She'd said she thought she was marvellous. The words sent a glow through the old lady. If only she could be sure that Tristan was all right.

Going off duty, Anna hurried along to Casualty before picking Emma up at the crèche. She must see Ron. She felt excited. He'd help she was sure, and she wanted to arrange it straight away. Ron was surprised to see her; he was also surprised to realize how pleased he was to see her. She was grinning like a Cheshire cat. He couldn't help smiling too.

'Ron ... can I have a word.' Ron walked along with Anna towards the crèche while she told him what she had in mind ... 'Do you fancy an outing tomorrow?'

'When?'

'In the split . . . in the afternoon break.'

Ron smiled, 'Why not?'

'Good.'

Ron waited for Anna to go on. But she didn't. She just pulled up her shoulders as though she was hugging some marvellous secret close to her . . . some lovely treat.

'Where are we going?'

'Not telling you,' she said, her eyes sparkling, 'It'll be fun . . .' She put on a reverent expression, to send up Ron and his Sally Army family, 'Doing good works actually.'

He gave her a playful slap on the shoulder, laughing. 'All right' he said . . . 'I'll find out, no doubt.'

They were almost at the crèche, and there at the door feeling very conspicuous was Bob Stetchley. Anna's step faltered for an instant and Ron sensing it, drew apart from her. Bob was looking him up and down. Bob was big, and muscley. He made Ron feel very small.

'Hi,' Bob said.

'Hi,' said Anna. She suddenly realized Ron was still beside her and quickly began the introductions. 'This is Ron,' she said . . . 'Ron, this is Bob . . . Bob works in the path. lab.'

'Hi,' said Ron. There was an awkward pause. Then Ron, feeling that three's a crowd added, 'I'll be going then . . .'

Anna's head turned to him, almost unwillingly. 'Yes' she said, 'See you tomorrow . . .'

'I won't forget,' Ron turned and went.

Bob had avoided Anna at coffee break and then again at lunchtime. He'd felt let down last night when she hadn't asked him in. He'd lain in bed unable to get her out of his mind, and this morning had awoken with every intention of laying off this particular woman. She was dangerous. But it was no use. He had to do something about her. It was the only way to get rid of her. If he made love to her, he was sure everything would be all right. She would recede to her proper place in his life. He would have got her out of his system. Well it was no use beating about the bush. She'd see through any move he made anyway, so he might as well get straight to the point. Anna, seeing him waiting at the crèche, knew it, so neither said much as he shouldered Emma and they started to walk to her flat. 'Got any booze in?' His question broke the silence. Anna wished she did have. She could do with a drink but she'd finished that bottle of plonk. She shook her head.

'Where's the nearest off-licence?'

'Round the corner.'

At the door, Bob dropped Emma to the ground. 'Now you are going to invite me in, aren't you?' he said quietly. Anna had been feeling pretty good already and his mood had sharpened her excitement on the silent walk home. Her eyes were huge as she looked at him. She didn't speak for a moment. She knew she was going to say yes.

'Yes.'

'What do you drink?'

She dismissed the usual plonk or lager and lime. She was going to need more than that. 'Scotch,' she said.

He inclined his head and made for the off-licence. Anna, feeling she had turned the corner and gone way past the point of no return, shivered.

'Mummy.' The weary, fractious cry of her daughter brought her back to her senses. There were things to do . . . practical things. She suddenly rushed the child upstairs. Yes, there was a lot to do and not a lot of time to do it in.

Emma, stunned into silence by the speed of her banishment to bed, uttered not one word of complaint. Anna could hardly believe it. She stood rooted to the spot in the sitting-room. It was as though her mind stood still. She had to keep reminding herself to get a move on. It was like talking to another person. There wasn't time to light the fire, so she switched on an electric heater, then just as quickly, switched it off again. Who was she kidding? She went into her bedroom and put a match to the gas fire, and turned on the bedside lamp. There was an atmosphere in the room. She stood and listened to it. The furniture spoke to her. It had come, all of it, from her childhood home, her parents' house in the country. The mirror reflected a different face, a sweet face, the face of a little girl. The chest of drawers bore the marks of her fingers, darkened round the knobs. The wardrobe had a stain shaped like a rocking horse where she had stuck a transfer. She'd scratched it off when she'd brought it to her new flat. Anna's fingers touched the stain, felt the roughness where the sticky glue wouldn't budge without scratching the wood. It might as well still be there, her rocking horse. It was all hers, the furniture, yet not hers. It was her past. When her father had died, her mother had sold the house and given Anna the furnishings for her flat, because Anna had nothing of her own. She had purposefully left everything from her marriage to Keith. It was His house, His furniture. It had never really been hers anyway. They were bought with his taste and his money. So Anna had been grateful for the hand-out from the old house. Only the bed was not the same. It had been her mother's and father's. It was made of walnut and Anna had always thought it magnificent as a child. Now, she saw that it was faded and the high polish of the bedhead cracked and scored with light scratches. How many unsatisfactory years had her father and mother lain there, side by side. The bed was sanctified by their sense of duty and by their sense of politeness to one another. It bore a rigid, staid expression, belied by the softness of its springs. Anna had felt a sense of guilt when she first lay in it; but she had enjoyed the guilt.

She sprawled luxuriously across it and knew that when they had lain there, her father and mother, they had dreamt about her; their only child, their future. Her mother particularly had centred her hopes on Anna. She had lain in that bed and planned the details of Anna's marriage, down to the number of *vol au vents* and cocktail cherries that would be required. Anna would shatter that dream, desecrate the sanctity of their politeness. She would do something that neither of them would approve of and enjoy every minute of it. Ghosts would also be laid tonight.

The knock on the door shook Anna out of her past. Again she felt rooted to the spot. A moment of panic fled through her. It was like losing your virginity all over again. She wanted to cry but stopped herself with the thought that red eyes are not sexually attractive. She went to the door and opened it.

'I thought you must have changed your mind . . .'

Bob, outside the door, had been having a panic too, of a different kind. He came into the kitchen and Anna got out some glasses. She held them while Bob poured the whisky. Anna was aware of the slight tremble of her hand.

'Bottoms up,' said Bob.

Anna drank the liquid like water and held out her glass for more. She giggled. The toast might have been more subtle, though perhaps less appropriate.

'Bottoms up,' she said. Her eyes sparkled. Bob suddenly saw the joke and laughed too.

'Are you hungry?' Anna asked.

'No. Are you?'

'No.'

Her hand reached out and touched his shirt. The fingers slipped down the silky cloth then were withdrawn again. They looked at each other for a moment. Suddenly, Anna was moving.

92

'Bring the whisky,' she said.

The whisky bottle lay half empty on the rug, lying drunkenly on its side. Anna woke. Emma was crying. Turning her head Anna saw that the clock read almost ten o'clock. Bob was still sleeping. His face looked like Anna felt, exhausted. She was feeling the exhaustion that follows total release from the accumulated dreams and frustrations of life.

Anna lay, listening to her daughter for a while then slid from the bed and went in to her.

Emma's voice came to her out of the darkness.

'Mummy ...' There was a question in the child's voice.

'Yes, darling. It's Mummy.' She crept in the darkness to the child's bed, her own old bed, and sat beside her. 'What is it?'

There was a pause then Emma said hesitantly, 'Are you all right?'

'Yes, darling. Why?'

'You were crying.'

'Was I?'

'Ever so loudly ...' Anna put her arm round her daughter.

'Were you having 'mares?'

'Yes that's it,' said Anna. 'All the nightmares coming out ...'

Emma took her mother's hand, as though their roles had been reversed. The little voice sounded almost maternal. 'Do you want to tell me about it?'

Anna recognized *her* mother in the question, and wanted to laugh. Her mother's brief spell looking after her granddaughter had left its mark. The snort of laughter was turned into a cough. 'You'd better wrap up ... you'll catch cold.' It was uncanny. Anna wound the eiderdown round her. 'I don't think I need to tell you about it now, darling. I'm not afraid any more.'

'Good.' They cuddled each other warmly under the eiderdown for a while.

'I'm hungry.' Emma voiced Anna's feelings exactly.

'Shall I get us something?'

'Yes.'

'What shall I get?' Emma and Anna thought. 'Milky drink?'

'Yes.' The reply was reluctant.

'And . . . fish finger sandwich?'

'Yes.' Definite enthusiasm this time. Anna bounded up and went into the kitchen. She was famished.

Bob heard Anna moving about the kitchen in the depths of his sleep. He stirred and opened his eyes, squinting at the soft light from the bedside lamp. He'd known she wasn't in the bed, even while he slept.

He looked for a while at her empty place, then reached over for the Scotch. He wrenched the top off and took a mouthful straight from the bottle He could smell something frying . . . he felt hungry. He waited for the food to appear.

Anna made two doorstep sandwiches, and sneaking past her own bedroom door took them into Emma's room. She crept back under the eiderdown and the two of them feasted, giggling like two schoolgirls in a dormitory. They were a pair of mates, both quite happy in one another's company and having no need of anybody else. Bob, in Anna's room, felt excluded. He could hear their voices. He was forgotten, his usefulness done. When the voices died and the door opened eventually, Bob's eyes were closed. Anna went quietly to the bed and touched him gently.

'Bob . . .' Her voice had the quiet urgency of one who wanted to wake somebody but didn't want to get blamed for it. 'Bob.' He opened his eyes and looked at her. Her face had a soft happy look about it and there was fun in the eyes. He'd felt angry but now the anger had gone and a plaintive little-boy voice said, 'I thought I smelt cooking.'

'Fish-finger sandwiches.'

'What!' Anna rolled on to the bed beside him and sprawled on top of him. 'They're really very nice. Emma was hungry. I'd woken her when I cried out . . .'

Bob smiled, remembering. He'd felt pleased at the time and he did again now. 'Yes, you did wail didn't you?'

Anna smiled at him and planted a kiss on his forehead. 'Thank you.'

His hand reached out to her body but she withdrew from him. She had been satisfied. She didn't want him any more. But he wanted her.

'Shall I get you one?' she asked.

Bob thought . . . puzzled, 'Oh . . . a sandwich. Why not?'

Anna, humming softly, made him a sandwich and brought it in. She watched him eat it and seeing her still hungry look, he fed her bits of the fish fingers straight into her mouth. It was nice. He enjoyed it. When he'd finished, they looked at each other. Then Anna looked away inspecting the rug. She wanted him to go.

'Can't I stay?' he asked.

'Not tonight,' she answered. 'I'm tired, it's work to-morrow, and I'm not sure I want my daughter to see strange men at her breakfast table in the mornings.' Bob raised his eyebrows at the 'men', sighed and got out of the bed.

'It's very late,' he said.

'Only eleven o'clock. If you're quick you'll catch the last bus . . .'

Bob *was* quick and in plenty of time for his last bus. But he didn't catch it. He watched it go when he was only yards from the bus stop, knowing that he wanted to walk. It was drizzling, an oily, dirty drizzle that made the pavements shine in the yellow street lights. He watched the slabs pass under his feet as he walked then, looking up, noted the halo of cobwebs made by a street lamp behind a tree, its wet twigs and branches bare of leaves. Walking made him feel better, calmed his uneasiness. Most women wanted him to stay, to sleep with them and he'd left them behind, knowing that breakfast together meant something else ... It signified a more permanent kind of relationship. A one-night-stand was just that. It did not entail the morning light. It was gone with the dark, like a dream, a fantasy. But Bob did not want this fantasy to disappear. He had wanted to cement it with cornflakes and toast and tea. It was this that worried him. He felt he had been used, and he was left with a desire for more; not necessarily more physical satisfaction though he wouldn't say no to that either, but more of her. She had not given herself. That was it. She had given only her body. That was unusual in women and very perturbing. She was still in his 'in'-tray.

Anna sprawled over the whole width of the bed, smoothing the creases in the sheets with her feet. She was free, free at last, free of her childhood, of Keith, of her parents, of herself. What a relief! She had even felt easier with Emma. Perhaps it was just the release of tension and nothing more. Perhaps tomorrow she would feel as though nothing had changed. But somehow she didn't think so. Anna raised her arm above her head and looked back at the bedhead.

She touched it with her fingers, feeling the cracks on the polish. She had reconsecrated this bed to another life, baptized it. Anna smiled. It was her bed, her life, and she would do with it as she liked. Her eyes closed and she was still smiling when, hours later, the drizzle stopped, and the moonlight shone through the old familiar curtains; her sleeping face turned to bathe in its light and her breathing was deep and very easy.

Chapter Seven

There was a new nurse on the ward the next morning, Katy Betts. Her final exams behind her, she felt she had authority and status, even if the results hadn't come in yet and she was still nervous of the outcome.

'So nice to have fully trained staff on the ward again.' Nurse Bowell had said when they met in the office for the reports. Katy had glowed. She grew two inches and heard the admiring sigh of the young Jamaican pupil nurse by her side. She would have to take her under her wing ... and, of course, the student nurse, Nurse Newcross, also a first year – although she looked more confident. Katy looked forward to teaching the junior nurses. It would be part of her job from now on. She looked forward to the day when the results came through, and she knew she had passed; then her number would come and she would be able to wear the uniform of a staff nurse at last. It was an ambition she had had for a long time, and at last it would come true. She had applied for posts already, but for now, she would fill in, bide her time, taking some of the load from the acting-sister's shoulders. If Nurse Bowell was only 'acting' sister, then she was 'acting' staff nurse. That was how she was being treated and that was how she intended to behave.

Granny Betts was thrilled to see her grand-daughter. Now she could really show off. She had been on the ward for some days now, knew the ropes and in the day room she ruled the roost. She had the telly on just when she wanted, except when Nurse Bowell came in and switched it off, and her conversation easily dominated the handicapped timorous residents around her. Mrs Lilley, put off by her loudness at first, had grown to like her ward neighbour. She, Bert and Granny Betts would sit side by side in the day room and talk. It was nice to have someone to talk to. And Mrs Lilley had a lot to talk about. They were doing up her house so she and Bert could go back home and look after themselves again. Mrs Lilley dreamt of the day when they would turn their key in the lock and walk in through their own front door. They were being very nice about the house, even if they weren't redecorating it as well. A pity that. Mrs Lilley had always fancied the bathroom blue with green fishes on the walls.

She'd seen a paper like that in a shop once, and she'd hankered after it ever since. Bert would like it. He used to be a fishmonger. It would remind him of old times. Never mind. 'Beggars can't be choosers,' she'd say. Perhaps they'd save up and get someone in to do it if she went on at him enough.

Katy was doing observations, or at least she was trying to. Every time she appeared, Mrs Betts called to her. 'Pssst . . . Katy.'

The hissing irritated Katy. 'You're not at home now, Gran,' she told the old lady. 'You're not the only one on this ward.'

'No need to snap dear,' Gran said, knowing the way to make her grand-daughter feel a heel. 'I was just wondering if your results have come through yet. Nobody tells me anything,' she added plaintively.

'No,' Katy replied, 'not yet.' And she went on to Mrs Nicholson to take her BP and temperature.

'Pssst.'

'Not again,' thought Katy. She ignored the hiss and went on pumping up the arm band.

'Pssst.' Sighing, Katy marched back to her grandmother's side.

'Now what?'

'Could I have some more milk in me tea, dear? You know how I hate to taste the tannin.' Katy took the cup and poured milk into it from the trolley, while Mrs Betts showed off to Mrs Lilley.

'Do anything for me, she would. She's a good girl,' she whispered loudly.

Katy heard, and coming back with the cup said, 'You lead the life of Riley on this ward, don't you?'

Mrs Betts put on a tired, distressed expression. 'Oh dear, no. You wouldn't believe it, Katy. I never get a wink of sleep. Her over there . . .' She pointed at Martha snoozing on the opposite side of the ward. 'She keeps us awake all night going on about her bloomin' sausages, and singing her head off . . . I don't know how people are supposed to get better in these places, I really don't. I'm exhausted, girl. The sooner I get out of here the better.' Katy looked at her grandmother sceptically. 'And the food . . . you wouldn't believe the muck we get served. Of course I know old people don't matter. We're just a burden.'

She began to cry and Katy looked heavenwards in despair. She'd heard it all before. She got it at home. That was one of the reasons why Gran had been brought in here. She'd run Katy off her feet when she was studying for the exams, gave her no peace. Now Katy and her mother needed a rest. What rotten luck that Katy should end up on the very ward they'd sent her granny! You just COULDN'T get away from the old lady. The 'Psst Psst' of her granny followed her like a poisoned dart wherever she went. It was hard to keep up your staff-nurse status with that going on. Even young Nurse Slater thought it was funny and laughed behind her back. But Nurse Slater liked Katy's granny. And that was another cross Katy had to bear.

Beverley confided, as usual, in the auxiliary, Nurse Jarmolinski. The Polish woman had been like ballast on Beverley's first ward. She had begun to depend on her rather a lot. She sided with the patients against Nurse Bowell in her quiet way. She'd even brought in a bar of diabetic chocolate for Mrs Lilley, knowing how she longed for something sweet. Beverley approved of her. She was a family woman. Her role as mother and wife came first, and people revolved around her as the pivot of her household. Beverley began to do the same. She just couldn't see why a lovely old lady like Mrs Betts should have been put out to grass there. She should be at home where she belonged.

'She's so proud of her grand-daughter, too,' Beverley complained, 'It's a shame. English people just don't care do they?' Nurse Jarmolinski said nothing, only smiled. 'You never see a black face on these wards do you?'

The auxiliary thought about it. 'No,' she said. 'You do not.'

'That's because we look after our own,' Beverley explained. 'We stick together. Everybody's dependent on everyone else. And that's how it should be. You don't get places like this in Jamaica.' They were in the sluice room, washing bed-pans, and cleaning trolleys. Katy came in soaking wet. Nurse Jarmolinski took one look at her.

'What happened to you, my darling?' Katy laughed.

'I tried to get Mrs Poole to drink her coffee.'

Even Beverley smiled. It was nice to see someone else getting it for a change.

'We should have warned you.' Katy and the auxiliary nurse were laughing.

Suddenly Beverley asked, 'Nurse Betts, you're a trained nurse. What do you think's best for old people?'

Katy's heart sank. She knew very well what was behind the question; her grandmother. Suddenly she swung round on her heel and walked out, tossing her reply over her shoulder, 'Euthanasia.

Beverley was horror struck and even more horrified to see her anchor, Nurse Jarmolinski, bent double, laughing.

'It's a joke,' the auxiliary explained . . . 'A joke!'

But Beverley didn't think it was funny. She just couldn't see what people found to laugh at on this ward. She bore a weight of guilt over what had happened to Mrs Carr and she resented the old lady for it. She didn't like her. She was stuck up, unsociable, pig-headed and selfish. She was also a nuisance. Mrs Carr didn't fit into Beverley's idea of family life. In Jamaica, Mrs Carr would have been considered plain eccentric, because she didn't *want* to be part of a community, part of a crowd. She actually wanted to be on her own. Beverley couldn't understand that. It upset her own sense of security. People were unreliable. They didn't always want what you expected them to want, or behave as you expected them to behave. It was unsettling, and Beverley didn't want to be unsettled.

So it was Nurse Jarmolinski that Anna approached over her plan. The Polish eyes sparkled with pleasure and there was a definite air of anticipation about the pair of them for the rest of that morning. Beverley noticed it and so did Nurse Bowell. Beverley felt left out and when Anna left for her afternoon break, persuaded the auxiliary to tell her all about it. When she was told, she realized why she had not been included in the plans. Rightly or wrongly, she felt that Anna blamed her for Mrs Carr's condition, and she was hurt that Nurse Jarmolinski should seem to be joining Anna in blaming her. She didn't like Mrs Carr but she didn't wish the old lady any harm and she would help if she could. She wanted to feel part of it, so she agreed to help.

Ron was waiting for Anna by the crèche door when she arrived for Emma, and she greeted him with an excited kiss on the cheek. It surprised Ron, that kiss. He felt she was flirting with him, leading him on, but where to? He hadn't forgotten Bob waiting for her, just as he was doing now, outside the crèche door. He felt faintly ridiculous and he didn't know why. But Anna and her daughter were excited. He couldn't resist their grins when they came out together, both looking forward to the little expedition. Anna handed Ron the *A to Z* and they set out for Queenstown Road, where they would find a stop on the 137 bus route.

Emma had never felt so close to her mother before. She seemed more relaxed, happier, and it made Emma feel happier too. She'd only kicked Graham once this morning. It was that midnight feast. It had been fun. It had brought them together. Anna felt it too. It was rather like an enemy who had turned overnight into a friend. She knew there were many ructions still to come, but at least they were both on the same side now and that was something.

They were both in on the plan, knew where they were going today, and both kept it a secret from Ron. It was a mystery tour to him, past Clapham Common, over towards Gipsy Hill and on to Crystal Palace. He wondered if they were going to see some athletics at the stadium. Anna laughed when he suggested it. She shook her head. 'No, I told you. It's good deed time.'

Ron was used to being sent up for his Salvation Army home. All of his family were in the army but, although Ron helped, and went out with his family taking hot food to the down and outs, he hadn't joined the army himself. Nor had they pressured him into doing so; and he took the ragging from the nurses in good part. As usual he just smiled, nodded and said nothing. He'd let her string him along and ask no more questions. He'd follow where Anna led.

She led him to a row of terrace houses, and, when they rang the bell on the door of 8B, he heard a dog barking. Emma jumped up and down. She could hardly contain her excitement.

'That's him!' she shouted. 'Tristan! Tristan!'

'Sh,' said Anna and the two exchanged conspiratorial glances.

'How on earth is she going to keep a dog in her flat?' Ron wondered, thinking the dog was a present for Emma. Mrs Gardiner opened the door and Anna explained the reason for her visit. She was a bit stiff. Anna saw what Mrs Carr meant but Tristan's constant jumping about must have ruined several pairs of the long-suffering woman's stockings, and she was, after all, perfectly ready to co-operate.

'Be glad to get him out of the house for a couple of hours,' she said, handing over the lead. Then off they all went again, back on the 137 to Battersea, and, at last, Anna explained the plan to Ron.

On Ward G8 Beverley was looking anxiously at the clock. It was almost the appointed time. She signalled to the auxiliary who was turning Mrs Nicholson with Nurse Betts, and went over to Mrs Carr's bed. The old lady half lay, half sat, staring vacantly ahead of her. Her book lay open but unread in front of her. Bev looked at the title. *The Life of Sir Richard Burton, the Explorer.* She wrinkled her nose. 'Who's he when he's at home?' she thought. She shook Mrs Carr gently and the old lady looked at her.

'Come on, dear. Why don't you sit up now? Have a look

at what's going on in the world ... we want to make your bed.'

Mrs Carr sighed and said tetchily, 'You've made it once already today.'

'Well, my darling,' the auxiliary approached her with a smile, 'we want to make sure you're comfortable, don't we?'

Mrs Carr sighed and allowed herself to be heaved into a sitting position.

'Come on now,' Bev encouraged. 'We want you up ... why don't you have a look out of the window? See what the weather's like?'

'No, no,' Mrs Carr moaned, almost crying. 'Why don't you all just leave me alone.' Nurse Jarmolinski caught the tears in her own throat.

'I know just how you feel, my darling,' she said.

Mrs Carr looked at her with some surprise. 'Do you?'

'I felt just like that when my Maria was born,' she sniffed. 'I felt so hopeless, just as though I wanted to die. Poor Jirji couldn't understand it. Men don't you know.' She blew her nose loudly.

Mrs Carr looked at her, frowning. 'Are you trying to tell me I'm suffering from post-natal depression?' she said.

Beverley looked at the clock, then out of the window. They were coming. She saw three people, two adults and a child walking down the side of the hospital. They had a dog with them.

'Come on, Mrs Carr ... get up!' she said forcefully.

'Don't bully me,' Mrs Carr was roused with annoyance and got out of the bed herself, without help.

'Look out of the window ... go on!' Beverley was grinning widely. She was beginning to enjoy this, and the auxiliary crowded in behind Mrs Carr to see.

'Ah look,' Nurse Jarmolinski cried. 'There he is! And

isn't her daughter a sweet little thing.' Emma was holding Tristan on a lead and Anna and Ron were looking up at the windows searching for Mrs Carr.

'Don't you see them?' the auxiliary asked.

'Whom? I haven't got my glasses on!'

Beverley rushed for Mrs Carr's glasses and put them on her so she could peer through the window. She saw two people, no three, for there was a child there too. And there was something jumping up and down. The eyes focused suddenly.

'Why it's Tristan!' she cried. 'It is! Isn't it? Oh!' She was beside herself. 'The dear little man.'

Tristan jumped up, pulling at Emma's tight hold on his lead.

'Look I think he knows me!' Mrs Carr clasped her hands together. 'What a wonderful surprise.' Her face was lit with joy.

Nurse Jarmolinski blew her nose, and wiped the tears away from her eyes.

'It's Nurse Newcross,' Beverley pointed out.

'So it is. And that nice young orderly from Casualty. How very sweet!' She waved to them and they all waved back. 'Are they engaged?'

'I don't think so,' Beverley said, staring out at them.

'Well they ought to be. He should make an honest woman of her. What a lovely little girl.' Emma waved up at the old lady. She liked Mrs Carr because she liked her dog and she'd given them an outing. Her face was at its most appealing.

Suddenly Mrs Carr swayed. The auxiliary caught her arm and eased her into the chair by the bed.

'Are you all right, my darling?' she asked.

'Just a little hot and dizzy,' Mrs Carr replied.

Beverley and the auxiliary got her back into bed.

'I'm going home soon. I hope they've told him that. I'm going home to my little boy. My Tristan.'

Nurse Jarmolinski looked at her anxiously. She didn't look well at all. She searched for something to take her mind off her discomfort.

'Why don't you read your book?' she said, placing it in her hands; she looked at the title, then at Mrs Carr. 'I don't know why he left her, do you?'

Puzzled, Mrs Carr watched the nurse as she went off to the day room, blowing her nose and shaking her head.

The incident had not gone unnoticed by Nurse Bowell. When Anna returned to the ward, she spoke scathingly to her, 'I hear you've joined the social services.'

'What DO you mean?' Anna asked innocently.

'The dog.'

'Oh that! Community nursing, Sister! It's the new trend.'

The irony was not lost on Nurse Bowell.

'Well, you can take your Mrs Carr her pill, for being so clever.' She turned to the medicine cabinet and unlocked it, searching for the bottle of tetracycline.

'What pill?' Anna asked. 'I thought she wasn't supposed to be ill.'

Nurse Bowell casually put the pill in a container and handed it to Anna. 'Oh,' she said. 'The path. lab. sent back a positive report on the last urine sample. Dr Choudry's prescribed antibiotics.'

Anna snatched the container from Nurse Bowell's hand and hurried to Mrs Carr's side. The old lady looked flushed and her eyelids were heavy. Brushing aside the thanks Mrs Carr tried to lavish on her, she poured a glass of water and gave her her pill.

'They've decided you're ill after all,' she said.

Mr Lilley had not turned up after his lunch, to sit as usual in the day room with his wife and Mrs Lilley was becoming very agitated. Mrs Betts, sitting beside her, tried to take her mind off things, and when Katy appeared with Nurse Bowell to do the afternoon observations, she put on quite a cabaret.

'Psst.'

The familiar hiss distracted Katy, and she had to count Miss Hutchins' pulse again.

'Katy, are you deaf?'

Katy sighed and tried not to look at the acting-sister. She felt humiliated by the constant demands of her grandmother.

'Psst,' Mrs Betts hissed again.

Nurse Bowell nodded at Katy when she looked at her and she got up to go to her gran.

'I'm supposed to be having a holiday from you!' she protested.

'Come and talk to us dear. We're lonely.' Her look took in the distressed Mrs Lilley.

'Gran, I'm busy.'

'Not too busy for me.' It was the old blackmail trick again. Katy knew it off by heart. 'That ointment they've given me's done my eczema no good, you know.' Mrs Betts shook her head at the ineptitude of her doctors. 'Can't you give me something else, eh, girl?'

'You can only have what the doctor prescribes,' Katy reiterated wearily.

Crossed, and in front of her friend at that, Mrs Betts retaliated loudly, 'Is that 'cos you've not passed your exams yet?'

'No,' Katy hissed at her, trying to back away. But gran was not to be put off.

'Well, look here, if you can't arrange that, how about arranging me a pair of new slippers, eh?' Mrs Betts displayed the turquoise furry pumps on her feet. 'These are proper worn out, look.' She indicated Mrs Lilley with her elbow. 'SHE'S getting a pair of shoes free! On the National Health!'

'That's different.' What was the use of explaining, Katy thought.

'They're so shabby though! Can't *you* run to a pair for your old Gran, then?'

Katy sighed. She was hard up. She gave her mother what she could from her wages, and she was still on a student's salary. It wasn't much. She couldn't tell her gran, because knowing her, she'd only let the cat out of the bag, for Katy had been forced to do a bit of moonlighting in a pub near the hospital. She was working as a bar-maid two or three evenings a week. How could she afford to get her gran new shoes? Anyway, Katy looked at them, they weren't so bad. A go with a bit of detergent and they'd be like new.

'No.' She was beginning to think she'd never get away when Nurse Bowell came to her rescue.

'Nurse Betts has other patients to attend to besides you, Mrs Betts,' she said.

Katy could have died when her gran replied in the raucous voice she usually kept for their Sandra, 'Some nurse she is! Anyway, what about me friend here? What about Mrs Lilley? She's eating her heart out here 'cos her hubby's not turned up. Thinks he's died, poor soul! Why don't you sort her out, eh?'

'In a minute,' Nurse Bowell retorted. 'We can't do everything at once. Behave yourself, Mrs Betts.'

At this the old lady really let go. 'Don't you lot care about anything?'

After the observations, Nurse Bowell went back to the office to ring G7, Mr Lilley's ward. It seemed that he had taken ill after lunch and had been kept on the ward, confined to bed. The doctor had been sent for immediately. It didn't look good. Nurse Bowell put down the telephone. What was she going to tell Mrs Lilley?

Chapter Eight

The news was broken in little bits. But it tasted all the more bitter for that, like a broken aspirin. Mrs Lilley could taste every little piece. She was told that her husband had had a slight setback, and that he was being kept on bed rest. He had to be quiet. Perhaps tomorrow she could go and see him. Fear chased Mrs Lilley through the night. She lay, her eyes open, thinking of Bert and waited for the news that was promised her the next morning after the doctor had been to see him again. If her legs were better she would have got up in the night to seek him out. But the next day would dawn eventually and what would be, would be. Perhaps they would have to stay in hospital a little longer. They had both been longing to get home, Bert even more than her. But if it was for his own good ... By the time morning tea came round, Mrs Lilley had resigned herself to another couple of weeks on the ward and was looking forward to visiting her husband as soon as possible.

It was a hectic morning. Nurse Bowell's routine had to be got through in spite of Mrs Betts *and* all the rest who were acting up this morning. Mrs Lilley wasn't feeling on top of the world, so they allowed her to lie dressed on her bed and snooze as she liked. She'd had a bad night according to night staff. Mrs Nicholson needed turning more often, and Martha's blood urea was still very high. If only they could get her to take a drink! They had got Mrs Saunders ready and dressed for the day room, so that was her sorted. Mrs Saunders had a rotary Zimmer, a walking frame with wheels

110

on, so that she could make her way, centimetre by centimetre, to the day room by herself. Others had to be wheeled in in wheelchairs, the blind had to be guided and others, afraid of falling, had to be encouraged and supported all the way, talked over the great hurdle made by the wire lead on the domestic's polishing machine. As Beverley pushed Miss Hutchins through the ward in her wheelchair, she noticed Mrs Saunders still sitting forlornly by her bed. She frowned and thought it rather odd. Nurse Bowell on the way to change the bag on Mrs Nicholson's drip noticed it too.

'What's the matter, Mrs Saunders?' she shouted across to her.

Katy looked up. She was with Mrs Carr, making the two-hourly check on her temperature. When she had noted and recorded the slightly lower figure on the chart Katy went over to Mrs Saunders.

'What's the matter, Mrs Saunders?' she shouted in her face. Her lips articulated the words very carefully, for Mrs Saunders was rather deaf. The reply was barely audible. It was as if the old lady was afraid to say what it was all about. 'Why aren't you in the day room with the others?' Katy went on. Again the barely audible whisper and the despairing look in the eyes; Nurse Bowell joined Katy as her 'staff' nurse put her ear to the old lady's mouth. 'Come again,' she shouted.

Summoning up her courage, Mrs Saunders raised her voice. 'She's pinched me bicycle.'

Katy couldn't believe her ears. Amazed, she looked at the sister. Then back to Mrs Saunders again. 'She's pinched your what?' she asked.

'Me bicycle,' came the reply.

'She says somebody's pinched her bicycle,' Katy said disbelievingly.

111

Nurse Bowell returned the look with raised eyebrows. Then the penny dropped. She laughed loudly. 'Oh. I know! She means her rotary Zimmer!'

Katy laughed. 'I had a crazy picture of her careering round the ward, hair flying and ringing her bell.'

The laughter brought Anna and Beverley to the scene.

'Who's pinched . . . your bicycle?' Nurse Bowell asked, giggling.

'Her.' The long, white finger pointed over to Martha's bed.

'Oh, no.' Anna remembered her first day and Martha's walkabout. She could be anywhere on one of those, steaming down the corridors, sending the walking wounded flying in all directions. And if anyone tried to stop her she'd lay into them like Mohammed Ali. She could be very strong could Martha. Nurse Bowell remembered a time when she'd knocked a student nurse out in the bathroom. Martha didn't like baths.

'You've taken everything else from me,' she'd scream. 'You might leave me me own smell.'

A quick search in the day room and the toilets disclosed no Martha Poole.

'All right. That's it,' Nurse Bowell took charge. 'I'll alert the porters. One . . . no, two of you had better make a quick search of the hospital. And stay together. It'll need two of you if you find her.'

Anna and Beverley left the ward at a sharp pace. Martha had not visited any of the wards, so the two nurses made for Out-patients. There was an ante-natal clinic in progress. Women in various stages of pregnancy were sitting, gaping. Something was going on in the consulting room. Anna and Beverley saw the rotary Zimmer left abandoned in the passage way and with a deep breath barged into the room.

Mr Robson was fending Martha off with an upturned

chair while a nurse cowered in the corner, a protective arm round a woman eight months gone.

'Martha,' Beverley shouted. But Martha didn't hear. She was systematically wrecking the joint.

'I don't want your lousy rotten sausages, anyway,' she screamed, hurling a bundle of patients' notes at Mr Robson. The papers fluttered in the air and the folder landed, splayed on the floor, its contents torn and scattered everywhere, the word 'Confidential' clearly legible on the cover.

'Martha!' Anna and Beverley bravely moved forwards towards the old lady.

'You're in the wrong shop,' Beverley said suddenly. 'This isn't the butcher's.'

Martha stopped and looked at the pupil nurse. Anna held her breath.

'They don't sell sausages in here,' Beverley went on. It was like pricking a balloon. Suddenly the crisis was over. Anna and Beverley went to their patient.

Martha looked confused, upset. She sounded almost apologetic. 'Just because they're with child, doesn't mean they should get extra rations,' she complained. 'Flauntin' the fruit of their sins ... look at her.' She pointed vindictively at the still cowering woman. 'She had the fun. She ought to pay.' The woman blushed and tried to cover the lump.

'I'm married,' she explained.

'That's what you say,' Martha sneered. 'I know better.'

A porter arrived with a wheelchair, and fury spent, Martha allowed herself to be gently persuaded into it and wheeled from the clinic. The consulting-room was wrecked: the desk overturned, notes scattered all over the floor and the consultant's cup of tea was spreading like an epidemic among the loose papers, seeping into the print, and obliterating the consultant's carefully considered prognoses and diagnoses. The nurse and the doctor looked at the mess in dismay. It would take all morning to sort it out.

As they wheeled Martha Poole past the still gaping row of women, Anna turned to the pupil nurse. 'Well done,' she said. 'You were fantastic.'

Beverley laughed nervously. 'I'm all right in a crisis. We had plenty of them at home when I was lookin' after our youngest; little blighters! It's the going on, day after day, in that smell I can't stand.'

Anna nodded.

'Soiled sheets and pants. I thought I'd get used to it.' Beverley thought for a minute. 'Do you think they can smell it?'

'Yes,' said Anna.

'I'll have to have a word with Dr Gould,' Nurse Bowell said as they sorted Martha out. 'We can't keep on like this ... she should be on Psychiatric.'

'She'd probably improve if she'd only drink,' Katy sighed. She gave Mrs Saunders back her 'bicycle' and the bright eyes said their thanks. Independence had been returned to her at last. She set off down the ward towards the day room.

'Take it slowly now,' Katy called after her absent-mindedly.

Nurse Bowell snorted. 'What did I say?'

Katy remembered. 'Oh.'

The two of them laughed.

'What did you steal her bicycle for?' Beverley was asking.

'What?'

'You heard,' Beverley shouted. 'Crafty old ... lady.'

Anna laughed.

'She pinched my garters!'

Anna and Beverley looked at each other. Their very first

114

day on G8. They had collapsed laughing on the floor while they knotted elastic round Martha's leg.

'You've got some new ones,' Anna consoled her.

'Ah, but it was them I wanted.' Martha didn't want any old garters. She wanted her own, and it was the same in the day room. 'That's my chair,' she shouted at a coronary victim. And she would not be appeased.

'There's going to be a showdown,' Anna whispered. So they moved the lady with angina and Martha settled happily at last in 'her' chair.

'What's the difference?' Beverley asked. 'They're all the same.'

'No, they're not,' Anna replied. 'She wants a chair she can call her own ... it's her proof that she's still alive, still matters.'

Beverley couldn't see.

'If people respect that chair, as if it was her property, they're acknowledging she exists.' There was a pause. 'Well, *I* know what I mean anyway,' Anna said.

'I'm glad somebody does.'

Beverley had known where she was, dealing with Martha Poole in the ante-natal clinic, but now she was all at sea again. She understood the need to get liquids down the old lady. That would bring down her blood urea and she would become less confused. She understood Granny Betts too, even liked her and joked with her. But she didn't understand why a chair mattered so much to Martha Poole, or why Mrs Carr preferred reading in bed to being sociable in the day room. Nor did she understand why Mrs Betts had been brought into hospital at all. She wasn't really ill. Nurse Betts just didn't seem to care. She'd let her own granny rot on this ward. It just wasn't right.

Going into the sluice with the usual bed-pan she surprised Nurse Betts having a cry. Katy turned away from her and

115

blew her nose. Respecting her need for privacy, Beverley said nothing for a while, but threw the disposable pan into the waste and waited, while Katy pulled herself together.

'So you do care,' she said after a while.

'Of course I bloomin' well care,' Katy snapped. 'The day I stop caring, I stop being a nurse.' She sniffed. 'Remember that!'

'Yes ... Staff,' Beverley said respectfully.

'Haven't you heard?'

Beverley shook her head.

'He's got phlebitis.'

Beverley frowned. It was obvious she'd got hold of the wrong end of the stick. She'd thought Katy had been crying over her granny.

'Who?'

'Mr Lilley,' Katy dried her eyes. 'She doesn't know yet. I've got to tell her.'

Beverley took a while to think this one out. Katy cared about Mrs Lilley, but not about her granny. It didn't make sense.

'Is it serious?' she asked.

Katy nodded.

'What a shame. They were really looking forward to going out. I suppose they'll have to stay in now.'

'*She* hasn't got phlebitis.' It was like a thunderbolt to Beverley.

'You mean, she'll still have to go ... without him?'

Katy nodded again. 'It'll kill her!' she said.

'Oh, that's really terrible.' Beverley tore a piece of paper from the roll and blew her nose. It would never happen in Jamaica.

It had been a bad day for Katy. Gran never stopped pestering her from one minute to the next. She felt quite demoral-

116

ized. There had been that business with Mrs Lilley when the old lady had been so upset. Katy had been the one to tell her because Nurse Bowell had been too busy chatting to Dr Gould about Martha Poole. Then later on, she had promised to teach the student and pupil nurses how to test urine for sugar. She had taken a sample from Mrs Lilley and they all went into the sluice room to watch while Katy did the test. Mrs Lilley's diabetes was under control now. She was on one morning pill of a hypoglycaemic drug, and a careful diet. As expected, the sample showed blue. She showed them the chart on the inside of the cupboard door.

'It would go bright orange if there was a lot of sugar present,' she'd said. She did another test using a test strip and showed the different sections, showing the amount of pH, proteins, sugar etc. Again the sugar indicator went blue. 'Now I'll show you what happens when sugar is present in high quantity. More than two per cent shows orange.'

Anna and Beverley were grateful to Nurse Betts. The sister never taught them anything. 'I haven't the time,' she'd say. 'I'm short staffed.' They'd get the dirty, routine jobs to do and never learn anything. Well, Katy intended to take her almost staff-nurse status seriously, and teaching was part of the job. In fact she was rather enjoying herself and at least she was out of granny's way for a while. She put five drops of the urine in the tube, rinsed the dropper and then put in ten drops of water. Reaching for a teaspoon, she spooned some sugar from a bag into the tube, with the liquid, then dropped in the agent.

They waited, watching the contents of the tube. It went blue, and stayed blue.

'That's funny,' Katy said. So she'd tried again. She emptied half the bag of sugar into the bed pan, took the five drops from it, then ten drops of water, then the agent. The liquid was about 95 per cent sugar.

'That should be bright orange,' she said, panicking.

Anna and Beverley smiled at each other. They thought it was rather funny.

Katy felt the colour rise to her cheeks. 'I just don't understand it.'

It just wasn't Katy's day. Mrs Lilley had gone back to bed, upset after she'd seen her husband, and Granny Betts had insisted on going to bed too, 'to keep her company'. Then she complained of feeling hot. Katy took away a blanket, and opened a window, very slightly. She couldn't let in a draught because of Mrs Nicholson. Then Granny had gone on about talcum powder. Katy's mother had brought her some that smelt of hyacinths. Lovely. She wanted some of that and it was just out of reach on the top of the locker.

'You can't have it,' Katy explained. 'It's perfumed. It would be bad for your eczema.' But Granny thought that Katy was just saying that to spite her. She called for the auxiliary to get it for her, and Nurse Bowell who happened to be passing had interfered.

'You can't have that,' she'd said firmly.

But Granny Betts was determined. She stretched and stretched. The curtain hung just in the way, between her bed and the locker. She couldn't see, but she felt her way, over the wood, to the tin. Ah, yes. She had it. She closed her fingers round it, drew it back, and after a moment's pause to recover her breath, emptied half its contents down her nightie.

'Ooh,' she called to Mrs Lilley, 'that's nice.' Then she was quiet for a while. It was so hot in that bed. She began to itch, a little at first, but it got worse and worse. That ointment they'd given her was no good. It was flaring up again. Mrs Betts pulled out her nightie in front of her, looked down the front, and screamed. 'I'm foamin',' she yelled. 'I'm foamin'.

Help, help.' Frantic, she looked round the ward for nurses. 'Never one when you want one,' she complained. 'But they're always pestering you when you don't.' She pressed the emergency bell behind the bed, and lay waiting, panting from the effect of her panic.

Nurse Bowell and Katy came running.

'I think I've caught something really awful,' she shouted. 'Oh, our Katy ... You'll answer for this in heaven ... sending me in here. Hospitals are germy places you know ... I could have anything ...' Mrs Betts was scratching furiously. Nurse Bowell drew the curtains round the bed and helped the old lady off with her nightie. She was foaming all right. Katy's eye caught sight of a tin lying on the bed. She picked it up and showed it to the sister.

'Tooth powder!' Nurse Bowell took the tin, and held it up in Mrs Betts' face. 'Did you empty this over yourself?'

Mrs Betts looked at it. 'Ooh, I don't know. Maybe I did.'

'You did it on purpose,' the sister snapped.

'No, I didn't. I thought it was me talc. Katy wouldn't get it for me so I got it meself ... only it must have been that,' she finished off weakly.

'Granny,' Katy protested. 'I told you you could not have the talc ... it's bad for you.'

'I don't know what they pay you nurses for!' Granny hit back. 'I'd be better off at home where your mother can look after me properly.'

An idea sparkled in Nurse Bowell's eyes like spring sunshine. 'Would you really, Mrs Betts?' she said sympathetically.

'Yes, I'm miserable here. You don't care ... she don't care,' she accused Katy. 'None of you care. I'd be better off at home. I would.'

'All right, then, Mrs Betts.'

Katy stared at the sister.

'You *can* go home. I'll ask the doctor for you and I'm sure he'll agree. We'd hate to keep you here against your will.'

Mrs Betts stared at Nurse Bowell.

'Here. You can't do that.'

'But you said it was what you wanted.'

Nurse Bowell rose from the bed and swung the curtains back into place while Katy helped her grandmother with her nightie. She was laughing to herself. Good old Nurse Bowell. Katy liked the acting sister very much. She'd backed her nurse all the way. She was a clever clogs. She'd even outwitted her granny.

Granny Betts stared after them dumbfounded. That wasn't what she'd wanted at all. Not really. Mrs Lilley leaned over to her, her eyes red from crying, and moaned, 'I'm going to be all on me own, if you go. All on me own.'

Chapter Nine

They were in the canteen at lunchtime. Bob Stetchley was toying with a piece of grilled fish and a salad. Barry Hodgson lit up in front of him.

'Do you mind?' Bob said. 'I'm eating my lunch.'

Barry raised his eyebrows and said nothing. The smoke rose above the table.

'What's the matter with you?' Bob went on. 'Don't you want to score goals on Sunday?' Barry and Gerry passed a glance between them. 'You're short-winded as it is!'

'Not scored yet?' Barry asked.

Bob stopped chewing for a second but didn't look up. He stuck his fork in a lettuce leaf and stuffed it in his mouth.

'He hasn't you know,' Barry said to Gerry Dent. 'Perhaps you should have a go.'

Bob looked up sharply, gritted his teeth against the unresisting lettuce and ground his knife across the plate. It set all their teeth on edge, and the plaice, as Bob lifted it to his mouth, tasted like cotton wool.

'Hey you're really up tight,' Barry eyed him. 'Tease is she?'

'No.' Bob drank a mouthful of water. 'She's not a tease.'

'I'm surprised you haven't made her by now . . .'

'Shut it.'

'You'll feel better when you do.'

'Will I?'

The irony in Bob's voice did not escape Barry. He leaned forwards and spoke confidentially over the table. 'Go on, Bob. You can tell me. You have, haven't you?'

Bob just looked at him and went on eating.

'He has,' Barry announced to the others at the table. 'You have. Haven't you?'

'Yeah. Alright!' Anything for a bit of peace, thought Bob.

Barry's hand was in his wallet in a second and the dirty five-pound note slapped across Bob's piece of plaice. Bob crashed his knife and fork on the table and picked up the fiver.

'Stuff it,' he said, thrusting it across to Barry. But he didn't leave go. His fingers held on to the note.

'It's yours, mate,' Barry said. 'You earned it.'

The note disappeared into Bob's trouser pocket and he got up from the table taking his plaice with him. 'I don't like nicotine and tar with my meals,' he said.

Anna saw him, sitting at a table by the open window. A nurse, her cardigan pulled up round her neck, protested by glancing from time to time at the offending draught. Anna sat opposite him and shut the window. Bob looked up ready to snap her head off, then saw who it was.

'Hi,' he said.

'Hi.'

You could have eaten the air between them with a knife and fork. The nurse glanced from one to the other then sucked noisily on her spaghetti.

'What did you do yesterday? I didn't see you.'

'Went out,' Anna replied.

'Ah.'

There was a no man's land between them, littered with the debris of unspoken thoughts. Each one had to be picked up and looked at carefully before a safe subject could be found.

'Get home all right?' Anna asked.

'Yes.'

'Good.'

Again the search, the frantic search for something that could be said.

'You're looking well.' Bob smiled at her, his jaw still for once because there was no chewing gum in his mouth.

Anna smiled. There was no reply to that, except ... 'So're you.' The nurse at the other end of the table snorted. Anna looked at her and couldn't help laughing. She'd caught her sleeve in her bolognese sauce and was trying to remove the stain with her paper napkin. Anna pushed her own across to her, and the nurse took it to wipe at the brown mark. Bob watched all this with some irritation.

'Serve her right,' thought Anna, 'for listening in.'

'When are we going to get together again?' Anna asked suddenly. 'Or aren't we?' It was all so easy.

Bob breathed a sigh of relief. 'Sure,' he said.

'I hope they coughed up.'

'What?'

'The fiver.' Anna enjoyed his embarrassment.

He laughed.

'You've got some real idiots in the path. lab.,' she said. Bob looked up.

'Oh?' he questioned.

Anna grunted in disgust. 'Yes. Some stupid kid with a couple of "A" levels. Really made a boo boo.'

'Why? What?'

'On a urine test. We've got an old lady with really severe urinary infection, running a high temperature, burning, in bad pain, you know ... and some idiot in the path. lab. sends back a report on the sample marked "negative". No infection. No bugs.'

'Perhaps that sample *was* negative.'

'That's what the sister said. And maybe that could have happened if the infection was slight. But it isn't. Another report came back saying she had severe infection.'

'Well. It's all right then.'

'No, it's not. That old lady had another twenty-four hours to wait before she got any real treatment. The infection got worse. She got weaker and she suffered all that extra time. That so-called mistake by the path. lab. could have given that infection time to attack the kidneys . . . it still might have.'

Bob was silent. He was wondering who had done the test. It could have been him. He hadn't had his mind on the job the last few days. 'Some stupid kid with a couple of "A" levels.' That's what she'd said. Well that put the tin lid on it. Now he was feeling really great.

'What's the matter?' Anna touched his arm.

'Nothing.'

'It can't have been you, anyway. You've got a first-class mind.' She was laughing, sending him up, not realizing what she was saying.

'Yeah,' Bob's voice was tense. 'Some stupid kid with a couple of "A" levels,' he thought. It could have been him. Well she was really making him look at himself wasn't she?

'Where did you go?' she was asking. 'Which university?'

'Brum.' The answer was automatic.' This job's a stop gap.'

'Ambitious are you?'

Bob said nothing. Yes he was ambitious. It was the same in everything he ever did. He wanted to be top. It was the same with women, sport and work. And if the job didn't offer enough of a challenge, all of his competitive instinct was channelled elsewhere. At the moment it was centred in sport, and women. The excess energy left over after a routine day in the lab. was burned off on the squash court, or the football pitch, run off round the streets of Streatham, or on a girl. But it still wasn't enough. He felt as though he was just playing around. The more energy he burned, the more there seemed to be. It left him with a frenzy, a burning desire to do something. He couldn't make out whether it was plain job dissatisfaction or Anna, or a combination of both. Supposing it was him who had made the mistake in the lab ... what had made him do it? Boredom or Anna? Which came first? Was it boredom with the job that had made him careless and think of Anna, or was it thinking of Anna that had made him careless and make the mistake? If he had made it. Bob took some fresh chewing gum from his pocket, put it in his mouth and started chewing. Looking at him searching for the answer through the window pane, his eyes focused on nothing, Anna realized this was not the man for her. There was something else on his mind. He was like a dog straining on a leash, and she wasn't strong enough to hold him even if she'd wanted to. No. She only wanted to play with him for a while.

'What football team do you support?' she asked.

The head flashed round with a grin. 'Wolves.'

'Why Wolves? I'd have thought it would be Chelsea or Crystal Palace or something.'

Bob groaned. 'No. Wolves,' he enthused. 'My home town.'

'Eh?' Anna looked puzzled.

'Wolverhampton Wanderers,' he explained. He was smiling and his eyes sparkled. She had got him back in the game.

That night there was quite a party on Male Orthopaedic. Norman was going out the next day. They'd let his leg down and the blood ran into it like a song. Anyway, it made him dance. Rose, coming on duty, laughed indulgently as Day Sister told them of his shouts and wails. What a fuss he'd made. Charge Nurse Stan Shilling gave her a sidelong look. This was not the Rose they had all come to know and ... love? She linked arms with him and wheeled round the ward to Norman's rendering of 'The Bluebells of Scotland' in double time, played on the accordion. Norman liked to see people enjoying themselves, and the ward wailed and whooped, while Stan tried to keep the noise down and watched carefully to see there were no accidents. He didn't want any more broken bones on his ward! The brown ale flowed. It was all good clean fun. Rose's eyes shone as the patients clapped her up and down the ward, and she knew that every one of them wished they were dancing with her. It made her feel good. Norman, resigned to including her on his trip, thought she wasn't such a bad lass, really. In fact she was quite canny. He could put up with her.

'Come on, pet,' he said, holding out his arm when Rose brought Jack his malted milk.

Jack shook his head as Rose curled under his arm.

'I could quite fancy you,' said Norman.

'It's the beer talkin',' Jack's mournful voice drifted over them from the next bed.

Rose looked at Norman. His eyes were innocent and lustful at the same time. Yes, he did fancy her. She was sure of that. She smiled.

'By, I can't wait to get this plaster off,' he said. She knew what he meant.

'You'll have to manage for a bit.'

'Do you think I'll manage ... with practice, like!' he winked.

Rose giggled. 'With a bit of help from your friends.'

Norman cuddled her.

It was nice, friendly.

'How did you break your ankle?' Rose asked him.

Norman thought for a minute. He was a bit puddled for thinking, for remembering details, but he strained to oblige. 'Oh, well now,' he said. 'I was at work ... in the power station, like.'

126

'Battersea?'

'Aye.'

'What do you do? Are you an electrician?'

'Better than that.' He yodelled, banging his chest for no apparent reason. It was uncomfortable for Rose but she suffered it till he settled back again. 'I'm an engineer.'

'Oh. What kind of engineer?'

'Electrical. What do you think, working in a power station?'

Rose shrugged.

'Mind, there are other kinds I have to admit.' He really was puddled. 'Anyway. Where was I? Oh, aye. I'm assistant engineer.'

'Only assistant?'

'Give's a chance. I've just finished servin' me time.'

'Oh.'

'I work mostly in the engine room, you see. Now one of me jobs is checkin' the circuit breakers.'

Rose looked interested, so inspired and thinking to oblige, Norman went on. 'Well, I was up on an elevation, looking at a circuit breaker for the auxiliary supplies, like, well, you know they have oil in them?'

'No.'

'Oh, well. It's an oil that's used to quench the arc.'

'What arc?'

'Oh, heck. It's an electrical arc, a current, if you like. It's hard to explain. It jumps from one point to another.'

'Oh. How does oil quench it?'

'Well, this is a special oil. It doesn't burn.'

'I could do with some of that for my chip pan.'

Norman looked at her, his faith in her interest dwindling for a second.

'Go on,' she said.

'Oh. All right. Well, the oil needs testin' from time to time to make sure it's not full of carbon, like.'

Rose looked as though she was still with it.

'Now what we use to test it with is usually something white, like a handy notice hangin' about the place. So you roll up your sleeve and dip the notice in and any carbon shows up black against it.' Norman checked Rose's face. He wasn't quite sure she was following, but still, he persevered. 'Now, when you draw your hand out like, it's got oil on it, and what probably happened is this. A bit of that oil will have dropped on to me shoe, and got on to the soles. Now remember I'm on an elevation.'

Rose nodded, her gaze intense.

'So where was I? Oh, aye. Now Battersea is a pretty old power station and there's stone steps, and if there wasn't there'd have to be metal ladders, because you've got to get up and down somehow.' Norman laughed. Rose didn't. 'Anyway, I'll have slipped on the step because of the oil on me shoe from the breaker, and landed a bit heavily on the next elevation.' There was a pause. Rose thought a bit then said, 'And that's how you broke your ankle?'

'Probably.'

'Oh.'

As she went past Jack's bed, she heard him mutter, 'Well you did ask.'

The next morning, the effects of the Newcastle Brown made Norman's leave-taking a rather subdued affair. Waving aside the offer of an ambulance to take him home, he hobbled to the bus stop and went the three or four stops to Battersea Power Station by public transport. His Dormobile was parked close by. It looked all right. Somebody'd had a go at his wing mirror, he'd have to replace that. But apart from that, it looked unmolested. He'd left it in the charge of

John Duckham, 4th engineer, a good bloke with his head screwed on. He said he'd keep an eye on it. Norman was about to unlock the door and climb in when he noticed there were curtains across the windows. 'Funny,' he thought. 'Squatters!' Prepared for the worst, he tried the handle. The door opened. Norman poked his head inside. There was somebody there all right. Norman scratched his head. It seemed a pity to wake him, like. A snort shook the body of the sleeper and John Duckham's head peered over the top of the sleeping bag.

'Norman!' he said. 'You're out.'

'Aye. Don't let me disturb you.'

John yawned. 'I'd just got off. I knew you wouldn't mind, Norman. I'm on nights this week. Well, I can't get any kip in at home. You know Penny's had a nipper . . .'

'Aye.'

'Oh, of course you do. You bought that pink rabbit didn't you? Well, she's throwing her weight around a bit, you know. And what with that and the baby crying all day, and next door getting rewired, there's no peace for the wicked.'

Norman scratched his head. 'Well, John, you're welcome to kip on for today, like, if you don't mind me. But I'm goin' on a trip tomorrow, and I've got new brake shoes to fit an' that.'

'Oh. Do you want a cup of tea?'

The two men sat drinking tea, then John settled back on the bunk and Norman got to work on the van. It wouldn't start to begin with. So he had to set up the charger; then once he'd got it going, he thought he might as well drive round to the motor spares place. This was going to be the sticky bit. John lay taut, gripping the sides of the bunk, as Norman tried to feel the accelerator through his plaster. It only came up to his knee . . . he'd not let them take it any further. They'd have had him in it up to his armpits given

129

half a chance, but it was difficult. The van jerked and jolted round the yard, until John's white face peered over Norman's shoulder.

'Would you like me to drive?'

'No,' Norman reassured him. 'It's not insured for anybody but me.'

'Where are you going?' John asked.

'Nortons'. The brakes are about finished. I need new shoes.'

John, his stomach upset from night shift and lack of sleep, gripped the back of Norman's seat. His knuckles were white.

'Go on,' Norman said. 'Get your head down, man. I'll not disturb you.'

Rose's contribution to the trip was to be the food. So after suffering Jay's morning toilet with the bed clothes over her head, and hearing the door bang as her room-mate went out, she was up and making lists. 'Baked beans – 5 tins, bread, butter, jam, sugar, tea, dried milk, what else?' Rose remembered how the smell of bacon frying early in the morning used to entice her from her bed in time for school. 'Bacon, sausages, eggs, sauce, fat for frying. What else? Pickled onions,' in case they stopped at a chip shop; he'd be impressed by that when he wanted some pickled onions with his chips. He'd realize what a good housekeeper she was. He'd be really glad he'd taken her on this trip. 'Packets of Chow Mein, curry etc,' she wrote. What else did people eat? 'Meat pies, frozen sprouts, dried spuds, tin of fish.' He'd want something sweet with his tea, though. 'Biscuits, cake, tins of treacle pud, chocolate.' Rose sighed. That would set her back a bit. Never mind, it was her holiday. She was going to the country, the real country, not just Battersea Park, but the real country where there were trees and grass and things, and maybe cows. And of course there would be Norman. She had visions of them sitting round the camp fire, Norman playing on his accordion while she fried bangers. Rose looked at the list again. 'Frilly nightie,' she wrote.

John Duckham did not get a lot of sleep that day. After helping Norman fit the new brake shoes, and sitting in the driving seat, pumping up and down on the foot brake for a while as Norman checked the fluid levels, he was dead beat and went home to his wife, baby and a couple of aspirins. Norman felt rotten about it. The poor beggar only wanted a bit of sleep, and he'd got up from his bed to help him work on the car. Norman thought it had been out of the goodness of his heart. John knew that he'd get no sleep till it was done and if he helped, it'd get done quicker. Then he was all ready to settle down again when by way of thanks Norman played him a tune on his accordion. It was the last straw. With a strained smile, John had left for home. He felt he had trespassed on his host's hospitality for long enough. He stopped only long enough to warn Norman about the delights of marriage and children, knowing that Norman was soft-hearted and any conniving cow could take him for a ride any day of the week. Then with a friendly pat on his plaster he'd gone. Norman reflected on what his friend had said. Perhaps he should just shoot off at dawn the next day, and not call for her. Then he remembered her hopeful little eyes and that stroppy chin and went, 'Ah,' to himself. He couldn't do that to her. And to make up for even thinking such a thing he jolted the van round to the garage and paid twenty p to use the vacuum. It wasn't a palace, but at least you could see the floor now. He hoped she'd be pleased.

Lugging three carrier bags up the stairs of the Nurses'

Home, Rose was not pleased to be shoved aside for Ron Frost as he bounded upstairs ahead of his girlfriend, to open the door to his room.

'Watch it, mate,' she bellowed.

Ron turned, and seeing Rose with her bags said, 'Can I carry your bags for you, Madam?'

Rose scowled. He was sending her up. He thought, like they all did, she was a bad-tempered bitch. Well, serve him right, he could carry the lot just for that. She handed over the bags. Ron took them without a murmur, and exchanged a smile with Anna who was persuading Emma to move herself in the same direction as her mother. It had taken a lot of doing to get Ron to invite her into his room. She was determined to get him a reputation. She saw with satisfaction the backward glance Rose gave her as she disappeared behind Ron's door, with Emma.

Since the business of Mrs Carr's dog, Ron and Anna had felt like fellow conspirators. It was a game they played, putting their fingers to their lips and giggling when they were together and anybody came near. The builders were having their lunch break, so it was quiet enough to hear Ron's records, which he played rather than settle on the bed beside Anna. She watched him, amused.

'When will the flats be finished?' she asked.

Ron shrugged.

'Have you put your name down for one?'

'Yes, I have as a matter of fact.'

'Who have you asked to share with?'

Ron laughed self-consciously then said, pulling a face, 'Rose Butchins.'

Anna howled with laughter. 'Does she fancy you?'

'No, I shouldn't think so. I don't want to be uncharitable.'

Anna guffawed. 'But it's hard imagining Rose fancying

132

anybody. I should think if she did she'd bang them over the head and drag them off by their hair.'

Ron hovered by the record player.

Anna patted the bed. 'I'm not going to seduce you, you know. We have got a chaperone.' She indicated Emma who was bouncing up and down on his room-mate's bed. Ron sat carefully beside his guest, and Anna took his hand like a schoolgirl on a bus. Quickly Ron took his hand away and looked intensely at the palm.

'What's the matter?' Anna asked.

'Feel that,' Ron said. 'Huge isn't it?'

Anna felt the pad on the joint of his thumb.

'That's called the Mount of Venus. Huge isn't it?'

Anna burst out laughing, rolled over on top of him and they landed on the floor with Emma bouncing up and down on top of them. She thought it was the best game ever since she'd started pulling Marjorie Timpson's bunches.

It was Fleur who had read Ron's palm. He had tried to help her, sort her out a bit when she'd been so down after her interview with Sister MacEwan. She'd been told she was going to be reported to Mr Hastings, the Director of Nurse Education. It was a serious matter, Fleur was worried and humiliated at the prospect. It felt like being back at school, on the carpet for sticking chewing gum under the desks. She balked at the idea of being treated like a little girl, and Ron was no different. He'd told her to organize her life more, like he did, make sure she always got her eight hours in; only went out when she was off or on a late the next day. Fleur felt resentful, it was all, 'Yes sir no sir, three bags full.' So she'd read his palm to send him up. She'd got him quite worried too. He meant well, she knew that, and she'd felt better for talking to him. He was a good bloke really. A bit up tight, Fleur thought, but kind and sympathetic.

He was no fool either. She'd only sent him up to boost her own ego. He didn't mind, and she *had* done something to organize her life. She'd been really rather clever. At first she'd thought she'd have to give up the drama club, give up her new bloke, Raymond Crouch, the pet-food executive, and just when she'd got him warmed up too. But no, Fleur had had a brain wave. If she didn't have to wait for buses in the mornings, if she only had her own transport to take her to work, she could get up three-quarters of an hour later. Now Ray would only have to get up two hours earlier to take her into St Angela's, and he was always complaining of boredom and under-using his talents in his job, so, it wouldn't kill him to drive her in in the mornings would it? Fleur approached Raymond with caution.

She brought the subject up after three hours' going through his lines over a bottle of white plonk one night. He was usually malleable when he'd had a few glasses of that stuff, and she'd buttered him up saying how marvellous he was in *Boys in the Band*, the play the theatre club was opening with next week.

'It's the way you walk,' she said, 'with a wiggle.'

He had looked at her without understanding.

Fleur explained. 'You playing a gay just shows up how virile you really are. It gets me the way you flaunt your hips in that part; anybody who wasn't really virile, really butch, couldn't do that and get away with it. Unless they *were* gay, of course.'

Raymond spent some minutes trying to follow the reasoning. There was something in it, if he could only see it. He sensed that, and it made him feel pretty good. He drank another glass of Riesling and savoured the taste of Fleur's skin. She squeaked.

'Love bites don't show on black skin do they?' he said. It was soon after that that Fleur had asked him about the car.

She got so tired, she said, she was afraid of falling down on the job. It was all through helping him, so couldn't he, just once, take her in? Tomorrow perhaps?

'All right. Just the once,' Ray had said.

But it wasn't the once. Every day but Saturday and Sunday, when Raymond lay in bed till mid-day, he got up, started up the Porsche and drove Fleur to work in style. She drifted into Casualty, the smell of leather and after-shave still in her hair, the scratches from his badly shaven chin smarting on her cheek. It did wonders for her morale. It helped her forget the hurt and humiliation she'd felt in Sister's office. 'I'm treating you like a schoolgirl,' she'd said, 'because you're behaving like a schoolgirl. But I'll tell you this, schoolgirls aren't expected to cope on their own in life-and-death situations. Nurses, however, are expected to do just that. If you want to be a nurse, if you want to be treated like an adult then you must behave like one. Take on the responsibility for your own life, Nurse Barrett. I can't do it for you. Learn to take the consequences for your own actions.'

Well, she was learning the hard way. In spite of the chauffeur-driven Porsche in which she appeared every morning, it was a subdued and thoughtful Fleur who got down to the job in Casualty. She'd lost ground, but she'd make up for it, somehow. Somehow she would show them that she could be depended upon.

Chapter Ten

It was lunch time when Alison Broughton came in. She was on her own and she crawled into Casualty, bent almost double with pain. She was sick in the waiting area, so they took her into a treatment room and tried to get her to lie down on the bed while they sent for the doctor. But she wouldn't lie down. She sat clutching her knees and rolling from side to side in agony. Sweat mixed with the tears on her face, and she breathed as though she'd just run a race. Fleur checked the pulse. It was very rapid. She and Jay stood by her, trying to calm her. There wasn't much else they could do. She kept screaming in a loud voice.

'For God's sake give me something . . . please . . .'

Jay couldn't look her in the eye. It made her want to cry. It was terrible to see such pain and not be able to relieve it. 'What's wrong with her?' she asked Sister MacEwan when she popped her head in.

Jean shrugged. 'Could be anything, renal colic, a stone . . . Dr Choudry's on his way. He won't be long.' She smiled encouragingly at the distressed girl. She was young, about twenty-two, and she spoke with hardly a trace of an accent. She sounded educated.

'I know what it is,' she gasped. 'It's renal colic. I used to be a nurse. I'm an S.E.N. I should know.'

Jean retreated, looking at her watch, while Fleur tried to take her mind off the pain. 'Where do you work?'

'Between jobs,' she moaned. 'Used to work at Queen Charlotte's. She groaned loudly. 'Oh God, this is terrible.'

Jay couldn't stand it. She went back to the sister's office.

'Can't we give her anything?' she asked.

Jean shook her head.

'Nothing that would relieve a pain like that. We could give her Paracetamol, but it wouldn't make any difference. We'll have to wait for the doctor. He'll prescribe something.' Jean looked at Jay sympathetically. It wasn't easy to watch someone suffering and just hold their hand. 'Is Nurse Barrett still with her?'

Jay nodded.

Dr Choudry came into the office first. He noticed Jay was looking upset and touched her shoulder. 'What is the matter with my favourite little nurse?' he asked.

'It's her. The woman in the treatment room. She's in a lot of pain.

'Well now, let's go and see,' he said.

Jean looked at her watch. 'All right if I go to lunch?' she asked.

'Yes. I'm sure we'll manage.' Dr Choudry looked at Jay. His eyes did not smile. They were so serious. If Jay had caught a single twinkle, they could not have held her like they did. She would do anything for him. She would be his slave. People joked about life too much, Jay felt. You ought to take it seriously. Like Dr Choudry and herself. Filling him in on the way, she went with the doctor to the treatment room, where they found Fleur still holding Miss Broughton's hand.

'I hear you're a nurse,' the doctor said, forcing down her knees. 'Come on. Let me have a look.' He examined her abdomen; it was tender all the way down to the groin, and when he touched her sides and her back she screamed out, 'Oh God. Help me, please. Help me. Please give me something for the pain.'

Dr Choudry smiled but there was an anxious look on his face. 'Come on.' he said 'Drop your legs over the side. Let

137

me check your reflexes.' Moaning, as though every movement was torture to her, Alison dropped her legs one by one over the side of the couch. Dr Choudry tapped the knees. The reaction was slow and unsure. Alison began rocking again from side to side. 'I think we'd better have a urine sample to test,' he said. Jay jumped to it, and Dr Choudry asked Fleur to fetch a catheter.

'Oh no,' Alison shouted. 'I don't want one of them.'

'We must. We must. If you're a nurse you know very well we have to check things properly. I'm going to order an X-ray.'

'Can't you give me something first. Please?'

Dr Choudry turned on his heel and went to organize the urethrogram in the X-ray department, while Fleur helped Jay obtain the specimen for testing. All the time the girl kept pleading with them. 'Please give me something. Please give me something.'

Jay couldn't stand it. She went away to test the urine sample and left Fleur to help Dr Choudry with the catheter. Alison struggled and kept bending over, so they called in Ron. It needed a man to hold her.

'It will hurt if you struggle. You should know better, if you're a nurse,' Dr Choudry told her. So Alison was still and just kept wailing, 'Bastards, bastards.' The dye was inserted into the bladder, and the catheter withdrawn. Then when she passed the dyed water out again, she was taken, crying and moaning, to X-ray.

'Why don't you just give me something?' she kept saying. 'You'll have to anyway in the end. Why don't you give it to me now. Please.'

After a while the pleading descended into abuse. Fleur stood by, holding on to her, saying as little as possible. There was something wrong. She was too insistent, this girl. Ron helped her wheel Miss Broughton back to the treatment room. Jay's test had found nothing except maybe too much acid in the water; it was suspicious. The girl had changed her tactics. She tried the charm on Ron. She thought perhaps he might take pity on her.

'Please,' she said. 'You don't like to see a woman suffer, do you?' But it was strange behaviour for a nurse. She should know better than to try to get round a nurse who was doing his or her duty. She knew very well that drugs had to be prescribed by the doctor. Even Sister MacEwan couldn't give her what she wanted. She was trying to get them into trouble.

Alison had been in Casualty for over an hour, and Sister Jean had come back from lunch. Fleur, hesitant after her dressing down, asked to speak to her. 'It's that renal colic case. She keeps on at us about giving her a drug to stop the pain.'

'We can't do that,' Jean said quickly.

'No. I know. But she's so insistent.'

Jean looked at her wondering what she was leading up to.

'I can't help thinking there's something at the back of it.'

There was a pause. The sister and the student regarded each other. Suddenly Jean picked up a small torch from a drawer in the desk, and went out to the treatment room. Ron stood aside as the sister approached the couch.

'Nurse Barrett here tells me you're very keen on having a pain killer.'

'Oh, yes. Please.' The voice was urgent. Jean nodded.

'Look at me, please.'

'Why. What are you doing?' Miss Broughton was immediately suspicious.

'I want to see your eyes, dear,' Jean had a tone of voice that you could not easily disobey. She was using it now. Jean shone the torch into the girl's eyes, but Alison blinked and

139

then kept on blinking. 'Keep them still, will you?' After a second Jean stood up and handed the torch to Fleur. 'Here' she said. 'Take a look.'

Fleur looked. The pupils were large and black, and stayed that way when the light shone on them. Suddenly Alison started to retch. Ron went to fetch a bowl, while Fleur held on to the patient. Dr Choudry was back in the office, waiting for the X-rays. He had already phoned the ward. They were getting a bed ready for Miss Broughton's admission. Jean went in to speak to him.

'She's certainly addicted to something,' she said.

Alison had been sick again. She was shaking now, and the sweat stood out on her forehead in beads. She fought with Fleur. She tore at her dress, and caught at her cap. It lay cock-eyed over one ear. But Fleur just said, 'No. No I'm sorry, we can't give you anything. Only the doctor can prescribe drugs.' And she kept on saying it again and again, calmly but firmly. Dr Choudry and Sister MacEwan were a little taken aback by her appearance when they returned; but Sister smiled at her and, straightening her cap and apron, Fleur smiled too. Jean's face was saying, 'Well done,' and Fleur knew it.

It was a good subject for teaching. Jean enjoyed explaining to Nurse Harper what had happened. Miss Broughton was a pethidine addict. She'd had some nurse training, that was obvious, or she wouldn't have known how to fake renal colic. Jean explained that pethidine was always given in the pre-operative period in a case of that sort. Miss Broughton knew it and she used the withdrawal symptoms she was suffering to help her fake the symptoms of a urethral spasm. She would go up to the ward as originally planned and Dr Choudry would order an I.V.P. to check her out, then once she was cleared from his department, she would be sent on to the drugs' ward under the psychiatric consultant. It was all very clear. Jay understood perfectly. Standing at the door of the office ready to leave, Jay hesitated.

'Was there something else?' Jean asked.

'Well, I just wondered if you'd explain something else to me.'

'Yes, of course. If I can.' She indicated the chair and Jay sat down again. 'Go on.'

'I know how to take blood pressure and everything,' Jay said, 'but I've just never understood what it means. Does that sound crazy?'

Jean shook her head. 'It's just the pressure exerted by the blood on the vessel walls.'

'But, you've got the same amount of blood all the time, haven't you?' Jean nodded. 'So how does the pressure change from systolic to diastolic?'

'The diastolic measurement is taken when the left ventricle is in a state of relaxation, and the chamber is filling with the blood, and systolic when the heart contracts and empties the chamber.'

'Then the pressure should read higher when the chamber's full, surely?'

'Ah no ... the other way around. Look at it this way.' Jay was looking very puzzled. 'If you put a hose on a tap, and turn the tap on. Right?' Jay nodded. 'The water is just filling the hose and flowing on. But supposing you squeeze the hose between your fingers. Immediately the pressure inside the pipe builds. Now the heart contraction is like you squeezing the pipe.'

'Oh, I see,' Jay's face was radiant.

'Then you let the pipe go and the water rushes on. Stop the pipe again and pressure builds ... see? That's how the heart pumps the blood round.'

Jay went out thrilled to pieces. She'd been trying to grasp

that for ages. Jean understood. It was always the most obvious things that escaped you. Jay's face expressed her thanks. The sister had taught her where her tutors in the school had failed. Jean didn't need, didn't ask for, more. She had done it, made the penny drop with a resounding clang. It was very satisfying, very satisfying indeed. It made you think, did that. 'Yes,' Jean remembered her feeling of impotence when she had phoned up to G8 to ask after Mrs Carr. She still didn't know how that old lady was getting on. 'It just made you wonder whether you were in the wrong job.'

When she went home that night, Jay felt happy. She was beginning to get on top of things at last. She enjoyed working on Casualty, and when she'd seen Dr Choudry's name on the notice board asking for baby-sitters, she'd put herself down for one night next week. She was sure he'd have nice children, well-behaved, probably pretty too. She was looking forward to it. She'd do anything for him, and it was such a shame. He'd lost his wife a while ago. She'd died from cancer and left him with two young children. He might have a colour television she'd be able to watch all by herself, and there'd be food. She wondered what his house was like. Somehow she could just see the Picasso Blue Lady on the wall of the sitting room and a smoked-glass coffee-table. You could tell so much about a person from their surroundings. There'd be books of course, and maybe records too. He was rather 'with it' in his way. Yes, it would be very nice.

Even Rose didn't upset her that night, when she came in late and started tossing her suitcase and clothes all over the room. She was going away for a couple of days but she wouldn't say where. Jay sat on her bed and watched her patiently.

'You can have the room to yourself for a bit . . . have one of your boyfriends in.'

Jay was horrified, but Rose laughed. She was in a funny mood was Rose, not like herself at all.

'You're not going to do your packing now!' Jay complained. 'I want to go to bed.'

For answer Rose turned her back and blew a raspberry.

The next morning dawned with a steady drizzle, but Rose was not put off. She looked out of the window, watching for the Dormobile in the early grey November light. She felt as though she'd been there a long time, waiting. There was still no sign of him. He'd said it was blue. Rose screwed up her eyes. Her heart had just begun to sink when a big blue van turned the corner into the hospital road. Rose saw it ambling slowly down towards the Home and with a whoop she picked up her case and a bag and ran downstairs.

Norman greeted her at the door with a chauffeur's salute, and she handed him the bags before disappearing back upstairs. 'Probably gone to the loo,' thought Norman, arranging her luggage in the small space at the rear of the van. Then she was back again, two plastic carrier bags in her hands and a bunch of daffodils.

'What's them for?' he asked.

Rose felt foolish for a second and Norman smiled, ruffling her hair. 'Come on, buggerlugs, we've not got all day.'

But Rose was away again. There was her bag and her duffle coat, and a couple of extra blankets from her bed. Norman was beginning to feel pretty irritated as he piled them in.

'Hey. What a tip!' Rose looked round the living space.

'You should have seen it before,' said Norman. 'I vacuumed it out in your honour, I'll have you know, and them bits o' curtains . . .'

'Curtains!' Rose guffawed. 'Wash rags.'

'Them bits o' curtains are a new addition.' Rose piled in beside him and they were off. To begin with, Norman's foot

143

slipped on the accelerator and they did a sudden jump forwards towards the wall. There was a pause.

'Can you drive?' Norman asked.

Rose shook her head.

'Pity.'

But they were soon under way and singing 'I'll tak' the high road and you'll tak' the low road' all the way along the A2. Rose got her comb and using a bit of the toilet paper Norman kept in the back of the van for emergencies, she played the accompaniment. She was enjoying herself already.

Anna was feeling quite happy too. Mrs Carr was a little better. They'd even persuaded her to sit in the day room for a while. She might not appreciate the company of her fellow patients but at least it meant she had a walk from her bed to the day room and back again. She could go to the toilet on her own, and the offending plastic sheet had been removed. She had dried up. For Anna it felt like a major achievement. This was better than being treated as a baby doll by her husband and her mother. Not only had she proved that she could earn her own living but also that she could do it well. She could be a useful member of society in her own right. She walked with Mrs Carr to the X-Ray department and sat with her while she waited to be given her I.V.P. Dr Choudry had promised to investigate her long history of infection properly. They were going to get to the bottom of it at last.

Mrs. Carr was sceptical. 'I'll believe it when I see it.'

Anna left her, promising to come back and collect her in three-quarters of an hour.

She had been put on making beds with Beverley this morning. Nurse Slater had the nuclear family on the brain. 'You'll get married again, won't you?' she said.

Anna shrugged.

'I mean you have got a little girl to think of haven't you?'

'Exactly,' Anna replied.

'A kid needs both parents,' Beverley persisted. 'I mean, don't you think it's a bit selfish to deprive her of a father.'

'Emma is not deprived,' Anna blazed. 'Who the hell do you think you are, saying that to me?'

Beverley folded the sheet, tight lipped. 'She needs security,' she said.

Anna threw the blanket at her. 'It depends what you think's most important,' she said. 'Freedom or security and I happen to think freedom's the most important for both of us. So there!'

'Honestly, you're just like a kid,' Beverley shoved the blanket on to the bed, but Anna did not take her end. 'You're all the same you whites, got no sense of family, or belonging. You're so scared of losing your precious independence. Well, I call it irresponsible.'

'Call it what you like,' Anna snapped.

'If you people would look after your own, just be proper families, there'd be no need for old people to be in a place like this.'

'I suppose you'd put an end to the welfare state altogether would you?' Anna sneered. 'You can't rely on families all the time.'

'Well you should! We're all dependent on each other if we admit it.'

'Mrs Carr wouldn't thank you for that. Some people value their independence. Sometimes your family system, your community bit breaks down then you really need the welfare state.'

Beverley, moving on to another bed, pulled back the covers and wrinkled her nose. 'What a pong,' she said. She pointed to the soiled sheet. 'This is where your system breaks down. Old ladies left alone shitting themselves. This is your welfare state.'

Anna pulled off the soiled sheet and threw it into the skip. 'You pays your money and you takes your choice,' she said.

'You're wrong,' Beverley wailed.

'No,' Anna replied, smiling. 'We're both right. It's just that we're talking about two different things.'

Beverley didn't understand. She was unhappy. Her values didn't fit in here. She missed Granny Betts. She understood her but not Mrs Carr and not Anna either. They were two of a kind. They'd really palled up that pair. Well there was a dance tonight, with a proper reggae band, and she was going. It meant travelling home but she was going all the same. It was her day off tomorrow. She wanted to go home, and she would.

Anna had had enough of the nuclear family. Perhaps Beverley was right in a way, but you can't rely on other people. Nobody can. Anna thought of Mr and Mrs Lilley. They had been married for fifty years. They'd lived and thought as a couple. Now they were to be separated. It was a bit late in life to learn to cope on your own. Mrs Carr had learnt. Mrs Carr preferred it and so would she, Anna. She collected the old lady from X-ray and wheeled her back to the ward because she was feeling a little weak again, then went off, late, to her coffee.

Bob bumped into her as she turned down the corridor to the canteen.

'You're late.'

'Yes. Had to take an old lady to X-ray.'

'Fancy a drink tonight?'

'I can't.'

146

'I could bring one round.' He waggled his eyebrows. 'Know what I mean?'

'Why don't we spend a whole day together,' she said.

Bob smiled. That sounded all right. 'When?'

'I'm off on Sunday.'

'Ah.' His voice expressed doubt.

'What's the matter? You don't work on Sunday, do you?'

'No but . . .' He bit his lip. Anna waited. 'There's a game . . . football . . .' Anna was about to go for her coffee. It was getting late. 'Why don't you come?'

'Don't fancy it.'

'What about Emma?'

'I thought it was time Keith did a stint. I could maybe get him to pick her up on Saturday night, keep her till Monday morning. I deserve a break. Anyway his girlfriend might as well find out what it's really like to be a wife and mother.' There was a glint in Anna's eye.

'Jealous?'

'What? Of Josie? You're joking. She's welcome to him.'

Bob havered. It was an offer he didn't want to refuse and he had a feeling it might not come his way again. On the other hand there were the lads, the team, he didn't want to let them down. Anna waited, impatiently.

'Can't you come?' he said at last. 'Just for a couple of hours . . . or so . . .' Putting it that way, Anna couldn't refuse.

'Will it be called off if the pitch is waterlogged?'

'It'll have to be pretty waterlogged to call *us* off,' Bob grinned.

'Then I'll pray for a monsoon.' Bob laughed. Suddenly Anna realized he wasn't chewing gum. Either he'd swallowed it with his tea or he'd stopped fighting something. But what? She looked at him with interest. He looked as though he'd just lost a battle. But who was the victor?

'Any of that whisky left?' he asked.

'Quarter of a bottle or so.' They both smiled remembering that evening. It was a good moment. Then Anna said, 'I'll do the food if you bring the booze. Lager and lime's my poison.'

'God almighty,' he said. 'OK.'

'Right. I'll give Keith a ring. Tell him his number's come up.'

'Good.'

'I might even go to the launderette. Wash the sheets.' Anna turned and walked off to the canteen. 'Sheets' – the very word had got Bob going. 'Hell,' he thought. 'Sheets, what a woman.' He felt very happy as he walked back to the lab. He'd even guarded his interests with the football team. 'Sheets' – the word held all the promise of a night of bliss. Suddenly Bob caught himself wondering why he couldn't come round tonight. He felt a possessive urge to know why and didn't much like it. 'Ah,' he thought, 'Emma of course. Not over the breakfast table.' Reassured, he shook his head, grinning. 'Sheets,' he said.

Chapter Eleven

Their first night was spent at Lydd, because there were two nuclear power stations just up the coast at Dungeness, 'A' and 'B'. 'B' was not yet in commission but 'A' carried 200 Megawatts. They'd probably see it in the morning. Rose was sorting out their bunks, while Norman enthused over the future of nuclear power.

'Well, all I know,' Rose answered, 'all I know is, I wouldn't want to eat any fish and chips round here.'

'Why?'

'Not if they catch the fish from this bit of sea. Hey,' she shouted, 'where d'you keep your sheets, Norm?'

'I could just fancy some fish and chips.'

'Norm!' Rose insisted.

'Eh?' Norman's mind was on higher things. 'Oh sheets. I don't use sheets. They only need washing every few weeks.'

'Hells bells,' Rose, hands on hips, frowned. 'Norm, you need taking in hand.'

'Hadaway wi' ye,' Norman said. 'What's for me supper, woman?' He gave her a playful smack on the bottom.

Rose rummaged in the plastic bags, 'There's pies, we could heat them up in the oven, spuds, and veg, or sausages, bacon and egg and that, like we had at dinner time, Chicken Chow Mein, a tin of spaghetti sauce and a tin of spaghetti . . .' She looked at Norman's face, he was not enthusiastic. Rose panicked. 'Pilchards.'

'Oh heck.'

'Curry.' Rose sighed. Then she had a brain wave. 'Beans!'

'Yeah. Beans. We could get some fish and chips and put

some beans on the top.' It sounded good, Rose had to admit. So off they went rollicking over the grass back on to the road, and into Lydd for a chippie.

It was a wild night. The sea lashed spray against the windscreen and the wind whistled through the gaps between the doors. Rose had imagined them walking down the beach in the moonlight, but there wasn't any moon. Still, it was nice when Norman put his arm round her in the fish shop and she'd snuggled under his coat.

'Two papers,' he said to the woman.

'I'm having a pudden,' Rose insisted.

'All right, all right,' Norman calmed her. 'No need to snap me head off.'

They were soon back at the beach, parked just behind the dunes. They sat on their respective bunks, and dug in while the beans plopped comfortably on the little cooker. Now and again they looked up at each other and smiled. This was the life. 'The freedom of the road and a canny lass for company,' thought Norman. 'A cosy caravan for two,' thought Rose.

'Will there be a huge white dome like in the pictures?' Rose asked.

'We're not at Brighton.'

'No, on the nuclear power station, you great nana!'

'No,' Norman got going again. 'You only see them when you've got fast breeders.'

Rose giggled. 'Sounds rude.'

Norman smiled but was not to be side-tracked. 'Did you know that from here, almost from this very spot, there's a cable goes under the sea all the way to France?'

Rose stared at him then remembered the pickled onions. She leapt up enthusiastically and wrenched the top off the jar. She used to eat pickled onions like they were sweets, when she was a kid. She stuffed two in her mouth and crunched on them, a rapturous expression on her face. 'Is that a fact?' she said. 'Do you want a pickled onion?'

'Aye,' Norman dipped his fingers in and sucked on the luscious fruit. 'Makes you think, does that, an exchange of energy between nations, France and England.' He pondered on the subject for a while and Rose hoped he had forgotten it. 'Mind you, it's not much use. In fact it's a bit of a white elephant really.' Honestly, once you got him on to something you couldn't get him off again, he just went on and on. 'No bloody good at all.'

'I'm dying to see the sea in the morning,' Rose said. 'I wish we could have got down here sooner.'

They would have if Norman hadn't wanted to make a detour to take in the 400,000 volt power station at Kingsnorth. He had a pair of binoculars, 'For bird watching,' he'd said, winking and going, 'Aye, aye.' Rose had giggled, then he'd focused them on the cooling towers, and she'd stared at the lines of pylons, marching across the fields, in ever-increasing numbers. They were like an army.

'Look at all them pylons,' she said.

'Feeders,' he corrected her.

'Who are they feeding?'

'You, me, the nation, pet. They carry electricity that keeps us all going.'

'Oh. There's lots of them going to the power station.'

'Daft head. They go FROM the station not to it. It would be like coals to Newcastle carrying power TO the station.' He pointed at the 'feeders'. 'You see them quads,' he asked. 'Look, there's twelve, each side of the tower in three places; well they're conductors. They carry 400,000 volts.'

'Fancy,' Rose said, and shuffled her feet. She wanted to see some cows, and the sea, and sand and that sort of thing. Sighing, she left Norman to contemplate the mysteries of electrical power and set about cleaning up the Dormobile.

Norman wasn't pleased when he saw her with the sponge and detergent.

'What are you doing?'

'Cleaning up. It's filthy.'

'Oh heck,' Norman said, and got in the driving seat, jolting her across the van when he took off. But she hadn't minded. She'd laughed. It was just his way. He was a rough diamond was Norman. She put her arms round him from behind, and she knew he quite liked it really because the corners of his mouth twitched and he'd shouted at her, 'Bugger off.'

It was idyllic, really idyllic.

Norman fought his way manfully through the beans, using some bread as blotting paper. Rose looked at the huge slab of bread he'd sawn from the loaf and made a mental note to get some more in the morning. He had a man's appetite, had Norman. Then he yawned.

'Eeh,' he said, 'I'm tired.'

Rose felt suddenly rather nervous. That was the standard invitation to bed, well if you were trying to be subtle it was, anyway. She knew that. Norman yawned again and Rose joined in.

He laughed. 'Catchin', isn't it?'

Rose smiled and wondered where she was going to undress.

'You know I'm really tired,' he said.

Rose began to be a bit worried. He sounded as though he meant it. 'You will be. It's only your second day out of hospital and you were in bed for quite a bit.'

'I should be stronger then, for the rest.'

Rose shook her head. 'Doesn't follow.'

'You should know. You're the nurse,' he said. He stood up, bending his head down to avoid a clash with the roof, yanked off his shoes and his jacket and letting out a roar and a shudder wriggled down into his cold sleeping bag. Rose felt she'd been rather left behind.

'Don't you wear pyjamas?' she said. 'No, don't tell me. They only need washing.' She was glad she'd had the fore-thought to use the public loo in Lydd. Well, there was nothing for it.

'Turn your face to the wall,' she ordered.

Norman did so, gently singing and laughing. 'Wall-flower, wallflower . . .'

Rose placed the pieces of dish rag as she called them, firmly across the windows, 'in case there are any tramps about,' and she set about undressing. She rather hoped Norman would turn and take a sly look, but he didn't. He was too much of a gent for that. In fact by the time she was slipping the frilly nightie over her head, he had stopped singing and his breathing had become very slow and steady.

Rose lay, her blankets from the Nurses' Home doubled round her. She felt a little cold and wondered if Norm had a hot-water bottle stashed away somewhere. Somehow she doubted it. She looked across at Norman. She could just see his bulk darker against the darkness of the Dormobile side.

'Norman,' she whispered. 'Norman.' His breathing chan-ged rhythm but he didn't stir. 'Norm, I'm cold,' she said.

It was no use. She had to do something if she didn't want to be refrigerated by morning. Rose got up, pulled on her socks, and a jumper and cardigan. Only the skirt of the nightie stuck out frothily from under the navy wool. Pulling on her bobble hat, Rose snuggled back into the blankets, curling up into a ball against the cold.

The wind was still howling when she woke. She wanted to go to the loo. She lay back thinking about it for a while. Norman was well away, driving them home. She wished she hadn't drunk so much tea with her chips. Her need made her feel cold and shivery. She got up, threw the blankets

153

aside, and put on her shoes. She looked ridiculous; she couldn't see herself but she knew she looked daft. She felt for her coat and put it on, then opened the Dormobile doors. The wind howled in, and sent the dirty cups flying. They rattled about the Dormobile floor and Norman woke. He didn't know where he was for a second and there was this unearthly wail outside.

'Must be the wind,' he thought. 'Blown the doors open.' Frowning he got up to close them, glancing across to his guest to make sure it hadn't wakened her too. Her bunk was empty. She'd disappeared. He went quickly to her bunk to pull back the clothes and make sure she wasn't there, but slipped on a saucer on the way, landing heavily and smashing the scattered cups with his plaster. The wailing came again. With a flash of inspiration he realized. It was her!

'What're you doing?' he shouted through the closed doors.

'What d'you think,' she snapped. 'By God but that wind's cold,' she cried.

Norman laughed quietly to himself. Poor old Rose, it was all right for men but women had to expose themselves to the elements if they wanted relief. He imagined what it would be like, that wind wet with spray from the sea lashing round the extremities. Rose burst in, her teeth chattering.

'By, I bet you're blue,' he said.

'Which part?' She stood at the door freezing to death. 'Gerrup,' she shouted, 'I can't get in for you.'

He held out an arm and she dragged him from the floor.

'God I'm cold,' she wailed.

'Go on,' he said. 'Get in my sleeping bag. It's still warm in there.'

Rose paddled through the broken crockery to Norman's bunk.

'I know,' he said. 'Better idea still. Why don't I open up the sleeping bag . . .' He unzipped it, 'pile all the blankets on top, and get in beside you.' He piled the blankets on top, while Rose 'Oohed and Ahed' at the lovely warmth inside his sleeping bag. Then he was in beside her, and they wriggled into a possible position. After a pause, they wriggled again.

'Your bum's in the wrong place,' he said, laughing.

'No it's not,' Rose yelled back. 'It's your knees . . . and your elbows, they get everywhere.' So they wriggled again till she was front to his back, packed like a pair of sardines and Rose moaned at the soft heat of his body.

'Your feet are like two pieces of frozen cod,' he wailed. Rose giggled and planted them firmly against his thighs.

'Mercy,' he cried. Even through his trousers he could feel their icy touch. 'Eeh, you're perished,' he said. She was warming up now. They listened to the wind howling against the van, and Norman was thinking it was a good job he'd seen to the cable on the hand brake when he did the brake shoes. Rose sighed. Her breath whistled past Norman's ear, and tickled it. He giggled.

'What're you laughing at?'

'You're tickling me ear,' he said.

Rose laughed and her fingers felt their way inside his jumper to crawl icily up his back. It made him shiver. But it wasn't just the cold. It was nice. His hand felt the length of her body, then he twisted round to face her. Again it was the knees and the elbows getting in the way, but with a little co-operation they found a mutually acceptable position.

'Hey. Has anybody ever told you what a really cuddly little body you've got?' Norman said.

'No,' said Rose. She was soon nicely warmed up, and there was one thing about Norman, once you'd got him on a subject, you couldn't get him off.

Keith was much the same.

'Well you see,' he kept on saying, when Anna phoned him about taking Emma for the weekend, 'I'd promised Josie I'd take her out. We've got tickets to be in the audience for the live recording of . . .'

'*The Money Programme?*' Anna suggested.

'No. Light entertainment actually.' He wasn't going to tell her what it was now.

'Emma would like that.'

'No she wouldn't. Anyway I've only got two tickets, and I promised Josie.'

'Get another ticket then.'

'Too short notice.'

'You mean you don't want her.'

'Well, frankly, Anna, yes. It is rather short notice you know and I was rather looking forward to Saturday night.'

'So was I,' Anna answered. 'Well, come on and collect her afterwards.'

There was a pause at the end of the line, then a sigh. 'If you insist,' he said, grudgingly.

Anna bit her tongue. She didn't want to make him hang up now, just through a fit of pique on her part.

'Good,' she said. 'When can you come round?' There was another sigh.

'We'd thought of having supper afterwards . . .' A growl from Anna soon changed all that. 'All right, all right. The show finishes quite early, nine-thirty, so I'll be with you by, say, ten o'clock.'

'Good. I'll look forward to seeing you then,' she said. They both put down the phone feeling that each had compromised.

'You're going to see your Daddy for the weekend,' Anna said to Emma.

'Oh good,' her daughter replied. 'Josie always gives me strawberry mousse, and ice-cream and proper sweets out of a box.'

'Sucker,' said Anna.

At least if she had Emma out of the way by bed-time, it wouldn't be so bad. They could wrap her up in a blanket and transfer her direct from her bed to Keith's car. It meant they'd have to stay in all Saturday evening but there was something to be said for that too. Anna looked round the sitting room. She would have to do something. It was all so dim and faded and unexciting. She wondered if the chimney was blocked off. It would be nice if they could light a fire in the grate. She looked up into the blackness, but could see nothing. Anna frowned, thinking for a minute, then remembering the newspaper somebody'd left behind in the canteen that morning, she screwed a few pages of it up and set light to them in the grate. The smoke rose as if by magic and disappeared over the roof tops of Battersea. 'Yellow pages,' she thought and got on the phone to a coal merchant, then another, then another. Eventually she found one who would deliver on a Saturday. Then there were candles to organize, flowers to buy and a couple of new lampshades would be nice. Lighting made all the difference to a room, but shades were so expensive. Anna staring at the ceiling light had an inspiration. She would get some paper lanterns, Chinese things, with tassels on the ends. Anna nodded. Yes that would do. The food had to be quick and simple because she had no intention of slaving over a hot stove all this weekend, but it had to be good. Perhaps if she didn't eat on Monday, she might just afford steak. It was the obvious answer. Anyway they had to keep their strength up, for what she had in mind, and it wasn't standing in the rain, watching football. It promised to be a rainy weekend. Looking out of the window Anna urged, 'Rain, you bugger!

157

Rain!' That pitch had to get waterlogged. After all he could play football any day of the week . . . almost.

Waking to the smell of bacon frying, Rose could not at first make out whether she could hear hail spattering against the windows of the van, or fat spitting from the frying pan. What's more she didn't much care. She sprawled over the now seemingly vast space of the bunk, now that Norman had vacated it, and eased out the crick in her neck. A sudden scream made Norman drop his spatula and come crashing over the broken crockery to her side.

'Me leg. Me leg,' Rose screamed writhing on the bed in agony.

'Cramp', she screamed. 'For God's sake, rub it!'

Norman helped her extricate her leg from the sleeping bag and rubbed her calf for all he was worth. Rose's moans crept down and down the scale, until she sighed and said, 'That's better.'

He looked at her anxiously. 'Are you sure now?'

Rose nodded and smiled. 'Did I give you a fright?'

'You sounded like a cow in labour,' he said.

'Ta very much,' Rose replied.

Norman went back to the frying pan. 'Do you like your bread dipped or plain?' he asked.

'Dipped,' she said.

The bread was crisp and the bacon slipped greasily out of the corners of the roughly-made sandwiches.

'Hey,' Rose said. 'You make great bacon sandwiches.'

In the pause between chewing, Rose heard the rain streaking along the sides of the van, smattering the roof. 'Nice day for ducks,' she said.

It was a day for driving, not walking. Rose, transfixed by the windscreen wipers squeezing the rain across the glass, felt all her resistance to life melt away. The rocking motion of the van sedated the usual reactions of aggression and defensiveness. She felt almost peaceful. Norman too was happy just driving. He liked being on the move, once thought even of becoming a long-distance bus driver, and he'd got used to the plaster a bit by now. He only jerked when he had to move off from first. It had made him stall the van in Ashford, at the lights, and he'd wished he'd put some more distilled water into the battery before they'd come away. Still, all felt right with the world. Norman was quite happy.

'What do you put when people ask you for your address on forms and things?' Rose asked. 'The Income Tax people for instance.'

'No fixed abode,' said Norman.

Rose laughed. It made him sound like a criminal or a tramp. 'Where do your mother and father live?'

'On an estate in Houghton le Spring,' he said. 'They've got a bungalow.'

'I thought they'd be gypsies.'

'No,' Norman laughed. 'You see they don't appreciate the advantages of living like this!' He was off again. 'I can park right outside me place of work. Think of that! I don't even have to get out of bed to make me breakfast.' He stuck out his arm. 'I can reach the cooker from where I'm lyin', quick shave with the razor, then open the door and I'm there. No buses or tubes or rush hours. It's smashin', man.' Rose was quiet, allowing him his head. 'It's common sense when you think of it. We want to take a lesson from the tortoise, carry your home about with you.'

Rose wondered what Norman's parents' bungalow was like. She'd bet it was centrally heated.

'If you have a breakdown,' he went on, 'you can just boil a kettle, make a cup of tea and bed down till morning, when you can either see to do your repairs or get somebody to do it for you.'

'How would the rescue service work?' Rose asked. 'You know ... when they tow you home.' There was a long silence.

'I'm not paid up for that,' he said. 'But it's an interesting point. How can they tow you home when you're home already?'

That had shut him up anyway. Rose grinned and looked out of the window. The rain was clearing. It would be nice to stop somewhere for their lunch, somewhere where they could see hills and sheep.

Norman found a place with a good view and put on the kettle for the mashed spuds, while Rose ploughed through the wet grass of a field to find somewhere sheltered from the road.

'She's a canny lass,' Norman thought. 'Really sensible type.' He felt himself softening towards her. Yes, he was glad he'd asked her to come. He didn't usually like women on his trips into the wild. They usually sprained their ankles or something daft like that just when they were being chased by an elephant through the jungle ... well a herd of sheep anyway. Speaking of which what WAS that shouting? Norman poked his head out of the van. It was Rose. He pelted across the field and found her in the far corner, hemmed in by a bunch of bullocks. The leader kept moving towards her and bellowing alarmingly. Norman realized that it might not have been properly spayed. And that was enough to annoy anybody. The others were just playing 'Follow my Leader'. No it was him, that black one with his head down and the angry eyes. Rose was white with fear. Norman put his fingers to his lips to tell her to keep quiet and imitating the bullock, got his head down and charged at the animal yelling his head off. Rose stared at him amazed. He looked back for a second.

'Run, you silly bitch. Run!'

160

Rose ran, looking back every now and again to where Norman, making tentative dashes at the bullock, was just keeping it at bay. When he saw her clambering over the gate he made one last charge at the bullock and then turned and ran like he'd been fired by nuclear fission. The bullock stopped a couple of yards from the gate and gave one last snort as Norman cleared its bars and landed panting with exhaustion, at the other side.

'My God,' he said. 'I'll have to give up the brown ale.'

It had given Rose a lot to think about had that. She was no longer altogether sure that she liked the country. The sparrows in Battersea Park never chased you like that. When you thought about it, they could have had just as good a weekend, flying up the M1 and back and spending the night by Battersea Power Station where he usually parked.

'Why do you like driving round the countryside?' she asked.

'Oh,' he enthused. 'It's great. Smell the fresh air, man.'

Rose sniffed, and smelt sodden raincoats, and decaying leaves. She shrugged. 'Well if you like it so much, why don't you go and work in the country?'

Norman thought for a bit, decided the pies were hot enough, then passing her one, answered:

'I've been thinking about that,' he said. 'I work for the wrong firm that's the only trouble. What I'd really like to do is to work for the Board . . . apply for a job on the district. Aye. Up on the Border.'

'What border?' Rose was startled.

'The Scottish border, man. It's smashing up there, moors and hills and farms. You can see for miles if you climb up one of them feeders you know.' He pointed to a pylon.

'I bet you can. But why would you want to do that?'

'See the lay of the land . . . stretchin' out in front of you. Smashin'.'

Rose was feeling tolerant today. 'Oh well,' she said. 'Whatever turns you on.'

Norman grinned. 'Oh, now you've torn it,' he said. His hand was under her jumper before she'd finished her pie.

They went on to Canterbury for the afternoon, and saw the power station, and the Cathedral, both from the outside, then made tracks for Kemsley, north of the city, opposite the Isle of Sheppey. They'd be sitting pretty there for an early morning drive back into London in time for Rose's shift. She'd gone on to days, so that meant seven-thirty at the hospital. 'At least,' Norman had said, 'there shouldn't be much traffic at half past five on a Sunday mornin'!'

It was light when they parked, in a rather more sheltered spot than they had the night before, after travelling over to the other side of the little peninsula in the hope of catching sight of Grain, a station that was not yet in commission, through Norman's binoculars. The coast was in any case protected from the sea by the Isle of Sheppey, and they found a nook, sheltered by two fairly high walls, just slightly inland. It was still drizzling but the wind had gone down, so when Norman rediscovered the beach umbrella his mother had once stowed away under the bunks in case he ever took her to the beach when the sun was shining, he erected it at a modest distance from the van, for Rose's convenience, digging its end into the earth to secure it and stacking rocks all round. Rose baptized it with due ceremony and they settled for the night.

They tried putting the mattresses on the floor this time. The bunk was so narrow and Norman's leg so unwieldy, it made life, and sleep, rather difficult and they both had sore necks from last night already.

'Can you not cut me plaster off for 's?' Norman asked.

'Can I heck,' Rose said shortly. 'I'm not havin' you back in there making my life a misery.'

Norman smiled. Eeh, she was canny.

So they laid the sleeping bag and the blankets on top of the mattresses and stuffed the bottom of the van door with coats to keep out the draughts and turned in. A man taking his dog for a walk after dark, saw the light go out on his way past, then filled with ozone, dog and man were startled to hear as they came back again, a voice out of the darkness cry out, 'Watch what you're doin' with that bloody leg!'

Chapter Twelve

The rain had almost stopped when Bob banged on Anna's door. Emma was still revving up her bed ready for Brands Hatch; she'd refused to settle and Anna hadn't been able to get the fire to take.

'Hi,' said Bob. Anna smiled, then laughed.

'The place is a shambles,' she said. 'I'd wanted it just right. Fatal!'

As they passed Emma's door Anna shouted through, 'Shut up and go to sleep, you monstrous child.'

Emma had only laughed. Basically her mother was in a good humour, she knew that, and so was she. Emma was rather looking forward to going to her Daddy's. She always behaved beautifully with him, for a price. Anna took Bob into the sitting room.

'I've been trying to light the fire.'

Bob looked round the room, and saw a paraffin stove in the corner. 'Got any fuel for that?' he asked.

Anna nodded and brought in a can. She watched from a safe distance while Bob poured some over the smokeless coal she had had delivered, lit a match, and leapt backwards. It lit the fire all right, after bringing down a fair amount of soot, but they soon got rid of that and the red glow spread among the pieces of coal, slowly and comfortingly.

'I've got some chestnuts to roast for tomorrow,' Anna shouted through.

Bob watched the spreading red. It was very relaxing; he felt tired, very tired. He hadn't felt tired for ages. He sat staring into the glowing hearth and yawned.

Anna, coming in with a huge casserole and baked potatoes, began to wonder if she'd done the right thing. If he was sleepy now, heaven knows what he'd be like with a heavy lining in his stomach. She banged the tray down on the hearth and Bob's eyes shot open.

'Oh, sorry,' he said. 'Must've dropped off.'

Anna laughed. 'I thought we might as well eat in here,' she said.

Bob went to open the bottle of wine he'd brought and poured Anna a glass. 'Here's to the weekend.'

'I'll drink to that,' Anna replied.

The evening did not go quite as planned. The lights were soft, and the fire glowed romantically, but Emma persisted in ruining the atmosphere with her constant calls for glasses of water and her questions. 'What are you doing?' she'd yell from her bedroom. When they'd refused to answer they'd found her peering at them from behind the door. Bob and Anna looked at each other.

'It's only till ten o'clock,' Anna said. 'Only an hour.'

'Why don't we play a game?' Emma suggested. 'To make the time go more quickly.'

'Good idea,' said Bob. So Emma went back into her room and dug out the expensive game that her father had given her the Christmas before. It had been a game he'd wanted for himself and no one had thought to give him it. It was called *Risk* and was all about High Finance. Keith was an accountant and really keen on the job. Emma had never been able to play it because she couldn't understand it and Anna couldn't be bothered to explain it to her. Bob took it from the child and spread it out on the floor.

'Where's your ex gone?' he asked.

'Huh. Search me.' Anna shrugged. 'He said he'd got tickets for a show at the BBC. Probably *The Money Programme* or *The Nine O'clock News* or something.'

Bob laughed. 'Come on, you and Emma against me.'

Bob's old competitive instinct was reawakened by the game. It was really him against Emma. She was in her element. Every time he shook the dice she hissed at him, 'Hate, hate, hate.' He loved it. And when her mother made some foolhardy move she reprimanded her. 'Mummy, he'll win if you do that. We'll lose. Mummy don't.'

'I'm living dangerously,' Anna replied. 'It's boring playing for safety all the time.'

Bob watched her staking her money wildly, while Emma pouted. 'The game is called "Risk",' he reminded her.

'What's "Risk"?' she asked.

'Taking a chance,' Bob answered.

'That's right,' Anna laughed. 'Your Daddy would be furious if he could see me now.'

Emma pondered for a while. 'It's a good thing that money isn't real,' she said.

'Yes,' said Anna. 'It's only a game.'

'You'll lose all that money if you put it there,' Emma went on. 'You'll have to throw dozens and dozens of sixes to win.'

'All right,' yelled Anna. 'Then I'll throw dozens of sixes! God you're just like your father. She's just like her father,' she said to Bob.

'Why?' Emma demanded.

'No sense of adventure.' Emma thought about this for a long time.

Bob had won three times and Anna and Emma only once. It was half-past-eleven and at last they heard the long-awaited knock on the door.

'Mummy says I'm just like you,' Emma smiled sweetly at her father.

'Oh?' said Keith. 'In what way, precisely?'

'She says you've got no sense of adventure.' Emma spoke

166

the words slowly and carefully, determined to get them right. Keith knew that that was exactly what Anna had said.

Anna and Bob lay exhausted in front of the dying fire.

'God,' Anna moaned. 'Sometimes I could strangle that little . . . darling.'

Bob laid his hand across her breasts and felt the gentle shape of her body, stroking her as though she were a cat.

'She's just like you,' he said. 'She likes to play the game her own way, doesn't she?'

Anna turned her face towards his; his skin glowed in the firelight, the live coals reflected in his eyes. Her skin crept, under his hands.

'Shall we go to bed?' she said.

On Sunday morning they woke curled round each other. It had been so gentle and peaceful the night before, when they had both been tired. It had sent them both swooning off into their sleep. But as Anna drifted back into consciousness and the knowledge that she didn't have to get up for Emma, she grew restless. She wanted something more. She looked at Bob's face as he slept. The jaw drooped and the eyes had a tired look about them. She wondered why he had stopped chewing his gum and decided she would ask him. She inspected his face and his body quite objectively. He was really rather beautiful, but he looked like a man who had given in. It was his spark, his fight, that had attracted her to him in the first place; she wanted it back. Her stroking hand stopped under his chin and she closed the mouth. Bob woke suddenly. Seeing her face, he smiled sleepily and forced himself to come round.

'Hi,' he said.

'Hi, first-class mind,' she said.

'What about the rest of me?' he asked. Anna, climbing on

top of him, began kissing him passionately. He struggled for a moment, then rolled her back.

'You like being on top, don't you?' she asked.

'In everything,' he said, smiling.

'You'll have to fight me for it.' And so Anna goaded him into fighting her, and it was very good, far more exciting even than the first time.

'They'll hear you in Brixton,' he laughed.

'Let them,' Anna yelled.

It was a marvellous day. The luxury of breakfast at mid-day with a man instead of Emma for company and then the change of the football game in the afternoon. Bob jogged on to the field. His body was so tight, so strung up, like a jack in the box. It was that Anna liked about him, the compact body and all the drive behind it. But Bob had lost something of his usual vigour.

'What were *you* doin' last night?' Barry Hodgson shouted hoarsely across at him. 'Get stuck into it.' And under his breath, so Anna wouldn't hear him, he added, 'fairy feet.' But Bob was a good player. It was just that for once he was a bit tired, as he explained to the lads afterwards.

'Your heart's just not in it,' Barry said.

'No,' Gerry answered for him. 'But I know where it is, eh, Bob? Just tell me when you've finished with her. That's all I ask. That's all.'

Bob grinned. He wouldn't be finished with her yet for a while.

Monday morning, after a night roasting chestnuts, drinking lager by the fire, a beautiful steak and another night in bed together, when he felt they were only just getting in tune with each other, he was surprised by Anna's extended hand at the door, and her, 'Bye, Bob. Thanks for everything.' Then came the peck on the cheek and he felt like a door-to-door sales-man who'd sold a little more than he'd bargained for and had run out of lines. His smile was hesitant, then the door closed. It was too early yet to go in to work. Bob went home and kicked around his flat for a while before going in. What was she playing at? he wondered. Just what was her game?

Anna was feeling very refreshed and ready for anything, even Nurse Bowell. Having seen her daughter safely stacked away in the crèche, she reflected with pleasure on her ex-husband's exhausted face when he had delivered her home. Emma had acted up more than usual. She was probably proving she had a sense of adventure, Anna thought, and a good thing too. She'd avoid the meringue trap if anybody would. She was her own person was Emma. Mrs Carr was her own person too this morning. She had begun to com-plain about the food; at lunch time the cabbage was over-cooked.

'It should be crisp! Crisp!' she said, and she had caught at Anna's dress and said very crossly, 'Do you know, that's been annoying me ever since I came in here. They've cut it all wrong, it won't ever lie properly.' She smoothed the neck with her fingers, shaking her head, and Anna smiled.

The main problem was Mrs Lilley. Dr Gould came up and said she was fit to go. But Mr Lilley was not and would not be for some time to come. It cut Beverley and Anna to the quick to see her sitting there by her bed, so forlorn, waiting for the ambulance. They wished it would come and the agony would be over for them at least. But still she waited, becoming more and more agitated.

'You're lucky,' Mrs Carr told her. 'I wish I was going home today.'

When she began to cry, Nurse Jarmolinski tried to calm her, but it was no good.

'I don't want to go home on my own,' she said. 'I can't face it. I won't be able to manage, I'll have nobody to keep me company.'

Nurse Bowell had to be sent for to sort it out. 'You're upsetting the other patients,' she said. 'Now try and pull yourself together. You've got your diet sheet haven't you?'

'Yes.'

'That's all right then.'

'No. It isn't.'

Nurse Bowell sighed.

'How long will Bert have to stay in?'

'I really couldn't say, Mrs Lilley. Doctor told you about his condition, now didn't he?'

'Yes. If only I could stay. Then I could visit him all the time, like he used to visit me in there.' Her head indicated the day room. 'It's not much to ask is it?'

'You couldn't wait to leave us a few days ago,' Nurse Bowell protested.

'Yes, but it's different now,' Mrs Lilley whimpered. 'Why can't I stay?'

'We need the beds,' was the brusque reply.

Mrs Lilley looked round. There was her friend Mrs Betts, they'd sent *her* home and *her* bed hadn't been filled yet. 'What about that one?'

'We never know what's coming in, dear. We might get two patients in from Casualty in the next hour and then where would we be? We always like to carry two empty beds if possible.' And that was that. Mrs Lilley blew her nose and said no more.

And Nurse Bowell, in this case at least, had been right. For in Casualty there had just been an emergency. An old woman, Maggie Bloch, found unconscious by a neighbour. She had spotted the milk bottles left outside and worried.

170

The bedroom curtains were still drawn and Mrs Bloch was always up and about early. The neighbour had a spare key to the house and let herself in. She found Mrs Bloch apparently asleep in bed. But she wouldn't waken and felt cold to the touch so, alarmed, she phoned the doctor, who immediately sent for an ambulance.

Mrs Bloch came in to Accident and Emergency, under the care of Charge Nurse Russell Potter. He ordered her temperature to be taken and it was found to be an unbelievable 27 degrees Centigrade.

'She should be dead,' he said. But she wasn't. Not yet. Suddenly he remembered Sister MacEwan's silver suit. They'd ragged her about it when she'd first brought it in. She'd bought it at one of those climbing gear shops and it was made of a kind of silver foil. It kept in the heat of the body. She'd stowed it away in a drawer in her office. Russell sent Ron round to her for it, and Jean came back with him, proudly bearing the silver suit. Dr Gould was very impressed; it certainly saved any further loss of body heat at any rate. He admitted the old lady immediately and alerted ward G8.

This was the second crisis of the day. Nurse Bowell rummaged through her drawers for the electric blanket, instructing her staff at the same time. 'Use a Hoskin's bed,' she called after the departing Katy.

'Why?' Beverley asked.

'In case she has cardiac arrest. It's no use pumping away on her breastbone if the bed gives under you every time. You need a hard bed, with a bit of resistance.'

Mrs Bloch was to be admitted quickly, so they hurried to get the bed ready and they were just in time. The old lady was wheeled in only an hour after Mrs Lilley's ambulance had eventually arrived to take her home. Beverley was set to sit by her and keep taking the temperature, and B.P. It was a responsible job. The temperature could not be allowed to rise more than one degree per hour or, Katy told her, hypoglycaemia might occur. That was something to do with diabetes. Beverley knew that and it was pretty nasty. So she had to report the readings on the thermometer regularly and turn off the blanket for a while if it showed signs of rising too quickly. Beverley was finding her feet, and thrown in at the deep end as she was, she felt if she could cope here, she could probably cope anywhere.

When Mrs Bloch showed signs of life for the first time, Beverley felt a real sense of satisfaction. She leaned forwards to smile into the semi-conscious face. 'Hallo, dear,' she said quietly. 'Welcome back.'

Jay, groaning at being wakened on her day off by Rose, as she stormed into their room that morning to change, did not make her room-mate feel very welcome. Which was a pity because Rose had something in mind which depended a good deal on her room-mate's co-operation. She knew she should wait till this evening, but she couldn't bear the suspense. Rose had to ask her now. She plonked down on to Jay's bed and shook her.

'Jay! Jay!' she said.

Jay rolled her eyes towards her and groaned.

'Jay. I've got a favour to ask you.' It was definitely not the time but she'd started now, so Rose went on. 'Come on, Jay.'

Jay sighed and sat up.

'You know I've been away for the weekend?'

Jay nodded.

'Well, I was with a bloke.'

The surprise woke Jay as no amount of physical shaking could have done. She looked at Rose in disbelief.

'What's so funny about that?' Rose said, belligerently. 'Anyway, I was. Well he lives in a Dormobile you see and it's a bit uncomfortable.'

Jay looked at her without understanding. 'The bunks are single and very narrow, and his leg's in plaster.'

Jay couldn't help laughing. 'What am I supposed to do about it?' she asked.

'You won't tell anybody will you? Promise. I don't want anybody to know. It's my business, right?'

'So why are you telling me?' Jay asked.

'I thought that if you were on nights this week some time . . . are you?'

Jay thought and sighed. 'Yes. I start on Tuesday. When's that?'

'Day after tomorrow.' Rose was becoming very excited. 'I thought that you wouldn't mind if I smuggled Norman . . .'

'Norman?' Jay was laughing again.

'If I smuggled Norman into the Nurses' Home for a couple of nights.' Rose ploughed on determinedly.

Jay stopped laughing and looked at her. 'Smuggle him in here?' she asked. 'Into this room?'

Rose nodded. Honestly she was thick sometimes.

'You mean, use my bed?'

'Well no. We could sleep in my bed, I mean we'd want to be together.' Rose felt suddenly very adult and sophisticated. She was really rather proud of herself and it was one in the eye for Jay Harper too.

'I don't know,' Jay havered.

Rose got up and finished dressing. 'Come on, Jay. It's no skin off your nose, is it?'

'I wash my hands of it,' Jay said, snuggling down under the bed clothes. 'Don't let him sleep in my bed though.'

'All right, I won't,' Rose snapped back. On her way out of the room, Rose stopped and managed a hardly audible, 'Thanks.' She hoped Jay wouldn't hear it under the bed clothes.

Norman was very surprised to see Rose at lunch time, and not altogether pleased. They'd phoned through to the engine room to tell him he had a visitor, and it had embarrassed him. He wondered if something had happenened to his mam and dad or something like that, or the police had found out his M.O.T. wasn't up to date. He tried to remember when it was due. Then he saw Rose. He stopped in his tracks. She was the last person he'd expected.

'Top o' the mornin',' he said.

'Hallo.' Rose smiled apologetically. 'I'm sorry to get you out of work.'

'It's all right,' Norman said magnanimously.

Rose felt the distance between them. Only a few hours ago they had been so close that she could say or do anything but now . . . He was wiping the oil from his hands on a piece of rag, and trying to put a hospitable look on his face. Perhaps it was the boiler suit. Something had come between them that was for sure.

'I thought you weren't due to go back till tomorrow,' she said.

'Aye, well. There was a bit of an emergency, like, you know how it is and I was the handiest bloke around.' He laughed. 'That's one of the *dis*advantages of living close to your job.'

Rose smiled. 'I've got a suggestion,' she said.

Norman put on a shocked look for her benefit and she laughed. 'How would you like to spend a night on a proper bed?'

He frowned. 'What do you mean?'

'Well, I thought you might like to spend a night with me, in a proper bed. That's all.'

Norman smiled. 'Sounds great.'

Rose could tell he was having to try to sound enthusiastic. Norman was looking for the snags.

'You see my room mate starts on nights, day after to-

174

morrow, so I'll be on my own. Well, it's only a single bed but it's bigger than a bunk.'

'Sounds great,' Norman said again. He was trying harder this time.

'What's wrong?' she asked.

'Nothing. It's a great idea.' This time he convinced her.

'I'll have to smuggle you in.' Norman chortled. He was beginning to like the idea.

'Hey, you nurses are a randy lot,' he said.

Rose grinned. 'Fancy me, then?'

'Not half.' Norman was grinning too now.

'See you then . . . Tuesday if not before.' Norman nodded. 'See you by the hospital gate,' Rose said, 'about six o'clock . . . I'll be off duty and changed by then.'

'Right.'

Rose hesitated. Somehow she expected he'd kiss her, but he made no move towards her. 'Right,' she said again, then turned and went.

Norman was in two minds as he ambled back inside. He'd been put out at first. What was wrong with his Dormobile? he'd thought. But she had a point. The bunks were a bit little. He'd been scared to turn over the last two nights in case he squashed her with his plaster. Yes, she had a point and it'd be interestin' to see inside a nurses' home. 'Smuggle me in, eh?' he laughed to himself. Aye, she was a canny lass all right. But that was the trouble. She was a canny lass and it looked suspiciously like she was getting a bit too keen. He didn't want to hurt her feelings, like, and she'd turned out to be such a passionate little thing. He'd not expected to see her so soon after the trip. It made him feel hemmed in, trapped, being sent for when he was workin', by a lass. I mean, you couldn't say no, like, when a bit of crumpet offered herself. She might be offended. He didn't want to hurt her feelings. It was a problem though. Either way he was

175

goin' to hurt her. If he said, 'No, I'm not comin' round to the Nurses' Home,' she'd be hurt and if he said, 'Yes,' and she got even keener on him, and thought by coming he'd proved he was just as keen on her, then she'd get hurt again. It was very involved; it was that. It made him go all fuzzy in the brain, confused. He shook his head violently till he heard bells in his ears. And blow me down if they didn't sound suspiciously like wedding bells.

Mrs Carr was being difficult again. Nurse Bowell stood disapprovingly by the doctor's side while he explained the simple little operation to the old lady.

'You see,' Dr Choudry leant forward and took hold of Mrs Carr's hand, 'your X-rays may not have shown anything but that doesn't mean that there isn't anything there. Now with your history of infection I think we should have a proper look inside. It won't mean cutting you open or anything like that, and it won't be painful. You'll have a general anaesthetic and be asleep the whole time.' He looked into the grey eyes of the old lady, drinking in every word, and knew that behind them was a totally obstinate person who was going to do what she wanted whatever he said. He smiled. 'We might find something that would help prevent these infections happening again?'

'What kind of thing?' Mrs Carr asked.

'A stone, lodged somewhere, trapping the germs, a little twist in a tube, something like that.'

She looked at him disbelievingly.

'Now I know you're a very intelligent woman,' he flattered. Mrs Carr smiled. She was pleased, and Dr Choudry was encouraged, 'so I feel sure that you'll see the sense in allowing us to follow the investigations through.'

Nurse Bowell shifted impatiently from foot to foot. Mrs Carr was going to say no. She was sure of that. She didn't know why Dr Choudry bothered about her at all.

'Anyway. You think about it,' he said: he patted her hand and stood up.

'Yes, Doctor. I will,' Mrs Carr said in her little girl's voice. Dr Choudry smiled at her and left.

Anna, who had been turning Mrs Nicholson with Nurse Jarmoliniski, watched the doctor go and went across to Mrs Carr. The old lady smiled up at her, sheepishly.

'Are you being a naughty girl?' Anna asked.

'I'm afraid they think I am,' she said. 'They want me to have an operation, you know.'

'I know. A cystoscopy. They just want to take a look at you. Nothing else.'

'Yes. It's very kind of them to offer, but I'm afraid I'm going to refuse.'

'You know, you're asking for more problems when you're older . . .'

Mrs Carr giggled, 'My dear. I'm eighty-five'.

Anna put her hand over her face. 'Sorry.' She had to laugh. 'What I really meant was that . . . you might become permanently, well, like you were on the bus.'

'Incontinent,' Mrs Carr called a spade a spade.

'Yes.'

'That's true. I might. Or I might get knocked down by a bus tomorrow.'

Anna said nothing.

'I'll risk it! I'm too old now to have strangers messing about with my body, and I've managed perfectly well all these years without doctors and hospitals. I don't see why I should give in to them now!'

Anna felt helpless. She knew that as a nurse she probably should try and persuade the old lady to have the operation and yet perhaps she was right. She was old to be having general

177

anaesthetics unnecessarily, and after all, it was her choice.

'I'm only a little bit leaky.'

Anna laughed at Mrs Carr's apologetic face. 'I'm going to miss you,' she said.

'Nonsense. You'll be all wrapped up in that nice young orderly, if you've got any sense at all, which I doubt.'

Anna frowned. 'What young orderly?'

'That one from Casualty. I saw you with him when you brought Tristan to see me.'

'Oh! Ron!' Anna remembered him suddenly. 'Yes. Why not?' she thought.

'Apparently I have to wait for Dr Gould to sign my chitty of good health before I can leave, but I should be home in time for the Schubert song concert on Radio 3 tomorrow night!'

'You're determined, aren't you?' Anna said.

Mrs Carr nodded.

'Tristan will be glad to see you.'

Mrs Carr beamed. 'Poor little boy. I have to think of him too, you see. After all he hasn't got very long left to live and he misses his mother.'

'You know,' said Anna, 'you're just like my little girl.'

'That sweet little thing I caught a glimpse of outside the window?'

'She's not sweet. She's a very determined young lady. And you're a very determined old lady. You're two of a kind, determined to have your own way at any price.'

Mrs Carr laughed.

'Still, it'll be worth putting up with her tantrums now if she grows up to be anything like you.'

The old lady was very pleased with herself. 'Flatterer,' she said, but she was smiling.

Anna wondered whether Ron was still on a split as she was. She hadn't seen him for a few days. Well there was one way of finding out. They could surely think of something to do for the afternoon together. She'd enjoyed that day in the park and she had some really good talks with Ron. He was an interesting bloke. He might be younger than Bob, but he had a wider experience of life and Bob's first-class mind, in one direction only, could be a bit limiting. Ron thought a lot and that was stimulating on its own.

He was surprised to see her come panting down to Casualty just as he was about to go off.

'Caught you,' she said.

'Just.' Ron was pleased to see her all the same. 'I was just off to the baths.'

Anna noticed the bundle under his arm. 'Swimming?' she asked.

'Yes.'

'Oh, let's come with you,' she smiled. 'Emma really should learn to swim and I bet you're a fantastic teacher.'

Ron was aware of the flattery. Anna was a little too enthusiastic, but he didn't mind. 'OK. Go and get your swimming gear. I'll get Emma and we can meet up at the bus stop.'

Anna was surprised how good Ron was. He was a strong swimmer. She liked the way his body heaved out of the water and plunged back when he did the butterfly stroke. Emma watched him awe-struck. It was most impressive. Ron was gratified by their admiration.

'Come on,' he said to Emma. 'Let's see if we can get you floating.'

Emma was gripping on to the sides at the shallow end. Suddenly she was afraid. Her courage had left her.

'Leave go of the sides.'

Emma let go and let him hold her up in the water. She felt helpless lying on her back, but he held her with one hand under her head and another under her body. Then he took the hand under her away and she caved in, splashing wildly, her mouth and nose and eyes full of stinging chlorinated water.

'Aah,' she gasped. 'Mummy, that was horrible.' She was about to cry, and paddled back to the sides where she gripped the bar again.

'There's nothing to be frightened of,' said Ron. 'Watch me. Come on, Anna, float with me. Show her it's OK.'

Emma watched as her mother and Ron glided out from the sides of the bath into the middle of the water. It looked nice. It looked free. She'd like to float like that. It must be very nice.

'Come on,' Ron encouraged her and took one hand while Anna took the other. They led her out into the middle of the shallow end. Ron took her legs and lifted them while Anna put her daughter's head back, and she held her hand under the head while Ron supported the body. They swished her about till she relaxed a little. Emma started to giggle. It was a nice sensation, quite heady. She felt so light floating on the water.

'Let your head go right back,' said Anna.

Emma let it go. A moment of panic was soon overcome and very quietly, Ron took his hand away. Emma didn't notice, but Anna did. She smiled a conspiratorial smile at him. Emma felt safe and happy. Gently Anna let the head drop further back into the water.

'Don't take your hand away, mummy,' Emma cried.

'No, darling. Of course I won't.' Anna winked at Ron. The head was being held by one finger now, the water taking most of the weight. Slowly Anna took the finger away. Ron and Anna held their breaths. She was floating.

They stepped back from her. Emma's eyes sprang open in horror.

'Stay just as you are,' Ron cried.

Emma caved in a little but righted herself.

'You're doing it. You're floating all on your own.' He laughed. The excitement was too much for Emma. She laughed, caved in and ended up in the water. But she didn't mind. She'd done it. She'd done it all on her own.

Chapter Thirteen

Rose was panic stricken. They *would* do it to her. They just would. Bastards! They'd changed her shift, and all because somebody's father was ill, and somebody else reported in sick and somebody else was suffering from morning sickness. It was too much. They really pushed you around. But nights! Of all the calamities to happen to her. Why did they have to shove her on nights now?

Then there was the dilemma, should she let Norman turn up and tell him then or should she pay him another visit? If she left it till he came, he might think she was sort of standing him up. He'd feel pretty fed up, let down. If she went to the station he might be annoyed with her for asking after him again. He hadn't seemed too pleased last time. On the whole it seemed better to go to the station. If you had to do something unpleasant, far better get it over with and the suspense was killing her.

Norman stood wiping the oil from his fingers on a rag.

'I'm very sorry, Norman,' she said.

'Oh well,' he said easily. 'Another time.'

'It might be a while,' Rose said. 'It all depends if I can get my room-mate out of the way, you see.'

'I understand.'

'You're being very nice about it.'

'That's the sort of bloke I am,' Norman smiled.

Rose wasn't sure. Why was he being nice? She began to torture herself wondering if he was really glad deep down inside that it had all been called off, or was he just like he said, being nice? Her intense little eyes stared at him and made Norman feel rather uncomfortable. She really was a passionate little thing. The hairs rose on the back of his neck. He should have taken warning from John Duckham and thought about that time she'd starting cleaning out his van! Sure sign that! Women! They were a dangerous lot. They had you in knots before you knew where you were. You're nice to them once and they want to tie you down for life.

Rose could have cried. She sensed he was backing away from her and she couldn't make out why. She hesitated before turning away.

'Well, tarra, buggerlugs,' she said, trying to smile.

'Aye. Tarra well,' Norman said, smiling and nodding his head.

He was about to go when she added, hopefully: 'For now, anyway.'

Emma had given her mother no peace since she'd been to the baths. She wanted to go again and soon. Just in case, Anna had packed her costume, and Emma's with a towel, and left it at the crèche with the sour-faced Nurse Radley.

'I'm not a baggage department,' she said.

'I wonder,' thought Anna. She crossed her fingers Ron would go as well. There'd be ructions all afternoon if he didn't. Emma had really taken to him. He was her swimming instructor and she wasn't going to let him get away without following up his tuition. She wanted to learn to swim properly, like he did, not like her mother who did an ungainly breaststroke.

'At least I CAN swim,' Anna retorted, and left her to it.

It was hectic on the ward that day. Mrs Nicholson had died in the night. It was no surprise and none of them had got to know her that well. Even Beverley didn't seem too upset, as long as they didn't have to lay her out or anything like that. But the night staff had seen to that side of things. There were only the belongings to get through and precious few of them there were too. Nurse Bowell emptied the locker and dropped the things into a plastic bag, locking them in an office drawer until she was free to go through them properly.

Meanwhile Katy hurried in with the amazing news that Martha Poole had actually asked for a drink! Nurse Bowell flew to the kitchen.

'What does she like best?' she asked.

'I don't know. She had a couple of sips of that orange squash before she threw it at me yesterday.' Katy had had to change her uniform, and was afraid the yellow stain wouldn't come out. Nurse Bowell got out the orange squash, filled a glass, and put on a plastic apron, 'just in case'.

'Come on,' she said.

Katy went with her to the day room and watched while Nurse Bowell gave the old lady the squash. Martha took it from her, quite docile she was. And they held their breaths while she took one sip, two, three. Then she paused and looked at them. They smiled encouragingly. Then the glass was lifted to the mouth again. They wanted to clap. It had made their day. Dr Gould would be very, very pleased. He had begun to think she would be with them for always. The glass was still two-thirds full when she pushed it back into their hands and wiped her mouth on her sleeve. Nurse Bowell forgot to reprimand her for dirtying the dress and set the glass on the table beside her.

'You might want some more later,' she shouted.

Katy and Nurse Bowell were positively beaming. Even the search for Miss Hutchins' dentures didn't upset anybody. They looked everywhere, in drawers, under the television where incidentally they found Martha's garters. God knows how they got there. Under mattresses. They found two stale sandwiches under one mattress. Stashed away no doubt from tea for a midnight feast and then left, forgotten. What with one thing and another it was some time before Nurse Bowell got round to going through Mrs Nicholson's things.

There wasn't much of any real value. Her two children were in Canada, and her husband had died years ago, so there was no one left now. Still she'd better check through in case the children wanted the stuff sent on to them. Nurse Bowell emptied the contents on to the desk and started sifting through. There were her dentures. Nurse Bowell wondered idly whether it was worth checking if they weren't Miss Hutchins', then dismissed the thought. There was a string of coloured beads, a hair brush, hair grips, two paperbacks – one romance, the other a thriller, both well thumbed. Then she found a dog's tally, and read 'Blackie' on one side with 'Nicholson' and some old address she must have lived at on the other.

Beverley came in to write in the Incontinence Kardex and looked over her shoulder.

'Is that a picture album?' she said. Nurse Bowell pulled it towards her and they opened it. It was only small, with half a dozen or so choice snaps inside. It opened at a picture of a couple in Edwardian dress, a little girl standing between them, holding a doll. They read underneath 'Mother and father, June 1899'. The next picture was a photograph that had been taken in a proper studio, against a potted palm. It had been coloured in by hand. It showed a girl of eighteen or so in her best dress. Nurse Jarmolinski crowded into the office to look and Beverley went to fetch Anna.

'Come and see these photos Mrs Nicholson had in her locker. They're ever so old.'

Anna came in and they all stood round the desk staring at the tinted faces and the stiff collars. A photograph of a bride

185

and groom followed on. The groom was in army uniform. The first world war it must have been and underneath Mrs Nicholson had written, 'George and I on the day of our marriage.'

Nurse Jarmolinski sniffed.

'Doesn't she look happy,' Beverley said.

'His collar looks a bit tight,' Anna replied.

Then there were two pictures, one of George and his wife with their first child in her arms. She was sitting and he had his arm round her protectively. There was a bit of the baby's hair underneath. 'Birth of Edward,' the caption read. Then there was another, Edward grown older and George no longer in army uniform and sporting a beard, and on the mother's knee was another child. This one she called 'James'.

A daughter had followed and a group of three children appeared with a dog. 'Blackie' no doubt, again carefully tinted, the boys in sailor hats and the baby in a shawl, sitting on a cushion.

'I thought she only had two children,' Katy said, coming in.

There followed a picture of Edward in army uniform. Second World War. Nurse Jarmolinski sniffed again. 'I bet he was killed, poor young boy.'

A picture of a silver-wedding group with one daughter and one son followed, then a family shot of her daughter's family, in bright modern colour sent from Canada and alongside it a picture of 'Jimmy' all on his own with a peace-pipe and an Indian head-dress. And that was all.

There was silence in the office.

'I can't even remember what she looks like,' Beverley blurted out. Nurse Jarmolinski was sobbing. Even Nurse Bowell sat silently before this story book.

'I wonder what happened to George,' Katy murmured.

'Died I should think,' Anna said. She picked up an old powder compact from among the debris of a life, and opened it. It surprised them with a tune. It was a musical box and it played 'I'll Be Loving You, Always . . .' Nurse Jarmolinski blew her nose noisily, and they all left the office to go about their duties.

Mrs Carr, waiting for the ambulance to take her home, noticed the subdued look on the nurses' faces. She had created blue murder that morning about her bloomers, when her clothes had been returned to her freshly washed and in a plastic bag.

'These are not mine,' she said. 'There was a neat darn near the gusset. These are not they. See for yourself.' And she'd held the offending garment up for their inspection.

'Maybe you had on another pair, Mrs Carr,' Beverley had sighed. 'Your darned pair's probably at home waiting for you now.' Her smile had irritated Mrs Carr considerably and she had given Beverley short shrift. Then they'd kept her waiting for this ambulance. She had itchy feet. Mrs Carr wanted to go.

'I don't know how long I've been waiting,' she complained to Anna. 'To tell the truth I wouldn't bother except that it will save me a bus fare.'

'Let me . . .'

Mrs Carr was furious. 'I'm not a pauper. I can pay my own way.' Then she'd softened. 'Oh, dear. I know you meant well.' She smiled and Anna smiled back. 'You all seem to be in rather low spirits today.'

'Yes. It's Mrs Nicholson. The lady who died last night.'

'Ah,' said Mrs Carr. 'I thought so. You know, you're really very silly.'

Anna was startled. 'Why?'

'The trouble with you doctors and nurses is that when

somebody dies you think they've insulted you somehow.'

Anna laughed. 'Yes. I suppose that's true.'

'You can't cure old age, you know. It's very egocentric of you to think you can!'

'Mrs Carr!' Anna beamed. 'You're a tonic.'

'I'm going to catch the bus,' the old lady announced. 'I can't wait any longer. I want to see my Tristan.' Anna smiled. 'I hope he's all right,' she added anxiously. 'Your neighbour seemed very nice to me. I'm sure she's looked after him very well.'

'Humph!' said Mrs Carr. 'You don't know her like I do! I shall give her something for looking after Tristan. Then I won't have to feel grateful to her.' A sudden thought came into Mrs Carr's head. She dived into her handbag. Anna stood back deeply embarrassed. 'No not money. I know you wouldn't be allowed that.' She pulled out a silver thimble, and held it out in the palm of her hand. 'Please do take it,' she said.

Anna bit her lip and put out her hand. 'You might be needing it,' she said, almost crying.

'I have a perfectly adequate metal one at home,' Mrs Carr said. 'Emma might like it one day when she's old enough to appreciate it.' Then without giving Anna further time to object, she strode out of the ward.

Anna felt the thimble in her pocket while she waited in the queue for her coffee. It had an intricate pattern of vine leaves all over it, a beautiful little thing. Mrs Carr must have used it so often when she was stitching away at the back of her tailor's shop. It had been part of her life. Anna was very moved by the gift. Mrs Carr had taught her a lot. She was going to miss her. She'd taught her to value her independence, because when it came down to it that's all there was in life. And a good thing too, Mrs Carr would have said. Her life was no meringue, that was for sure. She could stand on her own feet, and so could Anna, and enjoy every minute of it. She could cope with her job, her life and even with Emma, and Emma in her turn would cope too.

She would see to that.

Looking round the canteen for a table, Anna saw Bob sitting on his own in a corner, reading a book. He was keeping half an eye open for her. She wondered why he wasn't with his mates. Purposely Anna turned her back and went to a table on the other side of the canteen. Bob saw and was hurt. He drank his coffee, determined to go out without a word to the bitch. But the way out took him very close to where Anna was sitting, so on an impulse he went to sit down beside her.

'Hi,' he said. Anna smiled and drank her coffee. 'Doing anything tonight?' he asked.

'Yes I am as a matter of fact,' Anna answered. 'I'm going out for a drink.'

Bob frowned. 'What about Emma?'

'Her gran's coming for her. She's been making her some new clothes. She wants to try them on her.'

'Oh.' Bob wanted to ask who she was going with, but didn't. 'Lager and lime, or scotch?'

'Lager and lime'll do tonight, I should think,' she smiled.

He felt he was getting warmer, but the climate was still far from summery. She drank down her coffee and got up from her seat. Bob was surprised. She'd only just come in, he thought she'd be staying for a while.

'I've applied for a job at the British Medical Institution,' he said. 'Research.'

Anna smiled. 'Good,' she said and she really meant it.

He walked along with her, out of the canteen. 'Time I moved on. This was only a stop gap.'

'I'm really glad.'

He smiled at her. 'Do you think you'll fancy me when I'm a Nobel Prize winner?'

'I don't know,' she said. 'Try me then.' The reply was the obvious one and yet it had shocked him. It sounded like 'Goodbye'. She was walking on a bit too quick for him. He took her arm and stopped her. He could not mistake the irritation in her face.

'Are you playing some sort of game?' he asked.

'Aren't you?'

'What do you mean?'

'I'm only playing the same game as you. That's all.'

'What makes you think I'm playing at all?' Anna looked hard at him.

'You were in the beginning. Remember?' Bob sighed. He did remember.

'All right. So I was playing a game but ... we've got to know each other now.'

'Look, Bob,' Anna stood aside to let some nurses pass. 'Bob, you said that your job was a stop gap. Well, you may not realize it, but so am I.' Bob tried to interrupt, but Anna ploughed on. 'And that's what you were to me. So let's not get heavy about it. You got me going again. I'm grateful. It was great. Now we move on. Right?'

You couldn't be clearer than that. She turned to go and he couldn't stop her. Looking after her he wondered if she was right.

The click of the staff nurse's knitting needles got on Rose's nerves. She looked at the clock. It was only eleven-thirty. There was the whole night to get through. She thought of those two empty beds back at the Nurses' Home and bit into her thumb nail. What rotten luck! Tonight of all nights. Before coming on duty she'd gone round to his Dormobile, but it wasn't there. He'd gone out. 'Carry your home on your back,' he'd said. Well, it made it hard to leave a message. She wondered where he'd gone, when he'd be back. She'd go when she came off in the morning, see if the Dormobile was there. Rose bit into her other thumb nail and got a black look from Staff. Looking at the empty space where his van should have been Rose had had a horrible sinking feeling. He'd gone. Gone for good, she knew it. Parked some other place where she couldn't find him. She could always call at the station, but it would hurt her pride too much to do that. His message was plain enough. He didn't want her pestering him. Tears stung her eyes as she thought of it. She got up and went to the sluice room to splash water on her face. Bending over the sink, her grief went through her like a pain and she cried out. Staff looked up from her knitting and after a moment's thought went in to her. But Rose didn't want her sympathy. She didn't want anybody's sympathy. She told Staff where she could go and what she could do with her knitting needles at the same time. She'd get over it, in her own way, in her own time. People did, didn't they? It had been nice to have a bloke, that was all, a bloke of her own, all her own. Rose sobbed. Perhaps the van would be there tomorrow after all. She made a cup of tea for a patient who couldn't sleep and bit off another nail. Yes perhaps the van WOULD be there. Perhaps everything was all right and this was just her imagination, her nerves playing her up. Perhaps . . . perhaps . . .

Anna, lying sprawled across the great expanse of her double bed, thought of the future. She used to be so afraid of it; but not now. Possibilities drifted across her mind. She would qualify, she was sure; be a staff nurse somewhere. Emma would grow up more monstrous than ever. Anna smiled, thinking of her terrible daughter. She'd be snoozing gently now at Granny's. She'd come through the divorce and out the other side and so had Anna. She was learning to swim. You never knew what the future held. It was exciting really, not frightening at all. And, of course, in the immediate future, there was Ron! Yes, Ron! Anna snuggled comfortably into her pillow. They'd had fun tonight. They'd gone out to a pub and found Nurse Betts behind the bar, measuring out the gin and tonics! They'd been sworn to secrecy of course. Moonlighting was not approved of. Anna giggled. Poor Nurse Betts; she'd find a way of sending her up about THAT tomorrow! Tomorrow ... What would happen tomorrow? Perhaps, if she was *very* lucky, she might get sent back to the right ward! But, she'd got a lot out of G8 she had to admit. She'd met Mrs Carr. Anna smiled as she imagined the old lady totting up the zzuzzs in her own bed, while Tristan lay across her feet, twitching dreamily. Good old dependable, independent Mrs Carr.

Anna's eyes sprang open. She switched on the light and looked across at the thimble on the bedside table. She picked it up and twirled it in her fingers. Why had Mrs Carr given it to her? It wasn't just so she wouldn't have to feel grateful to Anna, was it? To guard her own independence? The silver glinted in the light. It was, you know.

Anna laughed. Yes, that was exactly why she had given it to her. The crafty old ... lady. She smiled as she traced the delicate pattern of the vine, engraved in the silver, with its leaves, and its tendrils, clutching for support at the empty air.